Mary Mapes Dodge

When Life is Young

A collection of verse for boys and girls

Mary Mapes Dodge

When Life is Young
A collection of verse for boys and girls

ISBN/EAN: 9783337057466

Printed in Europe, USA, Canada, Australia, Japan

Cover: Foto ©Andreas Hilbeck / pixelio.de

More available books at **www.hansebooks.com**

WHEN LIFE IS YOUNG

A COLLECTION OF VERSE
FOR BOYS AND GIRLS

BY

MARY MAPES DODGE

AUTHOR OF "HANS BRINKER"
"DONALD AND DOROTHY"
"RHYMES AND JINGLES"
ETC., ETC.

NEW YORK
THE CENTURY CO.
1894

THE DE VINNE PRESS.

AUTHOR'S NOTE

Many of the verses brought together in this book originally appeared in " St. Nicholas,"— some of them unsigned, some under various pen-names, and others under the initials M. M. D. The rest are now printed for the first time.

Acknowledgment is due to Mr. Frank French, and to his publisher, Mr. C. Klackner, for the frontispiece, which so fitly illustrates the happy days when life is young.

CONTENTS

xii CONTENTS

WHEN LIFE IS YOUNG

THE MINUET

GRANDMA told me all about it,
Told me, so I could n't doubt it,
  How she danced — my grandma danced! -
      Long ago.
How she held her pretty head,
How her dainty skirt she spread,
Turning out her little toes;
How she slowly leaned and rose —
      Long ago.

Grandma's hair was bright and sunny;
Dimpled cheeks, too — ah, how funny! —
Really quite a pretty girl,
Long ago.
Bless her! why, she wears a cap,
Grandma does, and takes a nap
Every single day; and yet
Grandma danced the minuet
Long ago.

Now she sits there, rocking, rocking,
Always knitting Grandpa's stocking;—
Every girl was taught to knit,
Long ago—
Yet her figure is so neat,
And her way so staid and sweet,
I can almost see her now
Bending to her partner's bow,
Long ago.

Modern ways are quite alarming,
Grandma says; but boys were charming —
Girls and boys, I mean, of course —
Long ago.
Bravely modest, grandly shy.
What if all of us should try
Just to feel like those who met
In the graceful minuet
Long ago?

"IN THE GRACEFUL MINUET."

Grandma says our modern jumping,
Hopping, rushing, whirling, bumping,
Would have shocked the gentle folk
Long ago;

No; they moved with stately grace,
Everything in proper place,
Gliding slowly forward, then
Slowly courtesying back again,
      Long ago.

With the minuet in fashion,
Who could fly into a passion?

All would wear the calm they wore
      Long ago.
In time to come, if I, perchance,
Should tell my grandchild of *our* dance,
I should really like to say,
"We did it, dear, in stately way,
      Long ago."

GEORGE WASHINGTON DANCING THE MINUET WITH SALLY FAIRFAX.

1*

"I 'LL WEAR THE SWEETEST DRESSES,— AND, MAYBE, HAVE A BEAU!"

A DEAR LITTLE GOOSE

WHILE I 'm in the *ones*, I can frolic all the day;
I can laugh, I can jump, I can run about and play.
But when I 'm in the *tens*, I must get up with the lark,
And sew, and read, and practise, from early morn till dark.

When I 'm in the *twenties*, I 'll be like Sister Jo;
I 'll wear the sweetest dresses (and, maybe, have a beau!),
I 'll go to balls and parties, and wear my hair up high,
And not a girl in all the town shall be as gay as I.

When I 'm in the *thirties*, I 'll be just like Mama;
And, maybe, I 'll be married to a splendid big papa.
I 'll order things, and go to teas, and grow a little fat,
(But, Mother is so sweet and nice, I 'll not object to that).

Oh, what comes after thirty? The *forties!* Mercy, my!
When I grow as old as forty, I think I 'll have to die.
But like enough the world won't last until we see that
    day;—
It 's so very, very, very, *very*, VERY far away!

THE BEE-CHARMER

A FRISKY little faun of old
　　Once came to charm the bees —
A frisky little faun and bold,
　　With very funny knees:
You 'll read in old mythology
　　Of just such folk as these,
Who haunted dusky woodlands
　　And sported 'neath the trees.

Well, there he sat and waited
　　And played upon his pipe,
Till all the air grew fated
　　And the hour was warm and ripe, —

When, through the woodland glooming
Out to the meadow clear,
A few great bees came booming,
And hovered grandly near.

Then others, all a-listening,
Came, one by one, intent,
Their gauzy wings a-glistening,
Their velvet bodies bent.
Filled was the meadow sunny
With music-laden bees,
Forgetful of their honey
Stored in the gnarled old trees;
Heedless of sweets that waited
In myriad blossoms bright,
They crowded, dumb and sated
And heavy with delight;
When, presto! — with quick laughter
Gone was the piping faun!
And never came he after,
By noon or night or dawn.

Never the bees recovered;
The spell was on them still,—
Where'er they flew or hovered
They knew not their own will;
The wondrous music filled them,
As dazed they sought the bloom;
The cadences that thrilled them
Had dealt them mystic doom.

And people called them lazy —
Knowing their wondrous skill —
While others thought them crazy,
And strove to do them ill;
Their velvet coats a-fuzzing
They darted, bounded, flew,
And filled the air with buzzing
And riotous ado.

Now, when in summer season
We hear their noise and stir,
Full well we know the reason
Of buzz and boom and whir —
As, browsing on the clover
Or darting at the flower,
They hum it o'er and over,
That charm of elfin power.
Dire, with a purpose musical
Jarring the sultry noon,
They make their sounds confusical,
And try to catch the tune.
It baffles them, it rouses them,
It wearies them and drowses them,
It puzzles them and saddens them,
It worries them and maddens them; —
Ah, wicked faun, with funny knees,
To bring such trouble on the bees!

CHRISTMAS

THEY put me in the great spare bed and there they
    bade me sleep;
I must not stir; I must not wake; I must not even
    peep!
Right opposite that lonely bed my Christmas stocking
    hung;
And in the big bay window a funny shadow swung.

I counted softly, to myself, to ten, and ten times ten,
And went through all the alphabet, and then began
    again;
I repeated that Fifth Reader piece — a poem called
    " Repose,"—
And tried a dozen other ways to fall into a doze;

When suddenly the room grew light. I heard a soft,
    strong bound —
'T was Santa Claus, I felt quite sure, but dared not
    look around.
'T was nice to know that he was there, and things were
    going rightly,
And so I took a little nap, and tried to smile politely.

    "Ho! Merry Christmas!" cried a voice; I felt the
        bed a-rocking;
    'T was daylight — Brother Rob was up! and oh,
        that splendid stocking!

THE CALL OF THE SEA

IT is all very well to be good, I agree,—
    To be gentle, and patient, and that sort of thing;
But there 's something that suits my taste to a T
    In the thought of a reg'lar Pirate King.

THE CALL OF THE SEA.

A PLUMP LITTLE GIRL AND A THIN
LITTLE BIRD

A PLUMP little girl and a thin little bird
   Were out in the meadow together.
"How cold that poor little bird must be
Without any clothes like mine," said she,
   "Although it is sunshiny weather!"

"A nice little girl is that," piped he,
"But oh, how cold she must be! For, see,
   She has 'nt a single feather!"
So each shivered to think of the other poor thing,
   Although it was sunshiny weather.

THE POET WHO COULD N'T WRITE POETRY

Mr. Tennyson Tinkleton Tupper von Burns
  Was no poet, as every one knew;
But the fact that he had his poetical turns
  Was well understood by a few.

"I long, I aspire, and I suffer and sigh
  When the fever is on," he confessed;
"Yet never a line have I writ,—and for why?
  My fancies can *not* be expressed!

"Ah, what avail language, ink, paper, and quill,
  When the soul of a gifted one yearns?
Could I write what I feel, all creation would thrill,"
  Said Tennyson Tupper von Burns.

A LION MET A LITTLE BOY
  WELL VERSED IN HUNTERS' LORE.
THEN SPAKE HE TO THAT WELL-READ BOY:
  "WOULDST LIKE TO HEAR ME ROAR?"

"YES, THANK YOU," SAID THE LITTLE BOY,
WHO SCORNED ALL PALTRY FRIGHT.
THE LION ROARED ; THEN ASKED THE BOY :
"WOULDST LIKE TO SEE ·ME BITE?"

"OH YES," REPLIED THAT PLUCKY BOY,
    WHO COOLLY EYED HIS GUN;
"BUT FIRST I'D LIKE TO TRY THIS TOY;—
    WOULDST LIKE TO SEE SOME FUN?"

THEN FLED THAT LION FROM THE BOY,
AS BEAST NE'ER RAN BEFORE ;—
AND TO THIS DAY THAT LITTLE BOY
ENJOYS HIS HUNTERS' LORE.

POOR MARIONETTE

POOR Marionette! She worked so hard,
And did her part with such precision!
But one cold day, when off her guard,
She tumbled on the cruel floor
And broke herself for evermore.
Then worthless quite —
Poor wooden mite! —
She met with scorn and cold derision.

"Throw her away!" the showman cried;
"Throw her away. We'll have a new one."
And so, despised and cast aside,
She lay all winter in the snow,
Unmourned, forgotten long ago
By human folk;
And never woke,—
So can a cruel fate undo one!

Poor Marionette! In course of time
Sweet May came, bringing balmy weather.
Then followed summer in her prime;
And softly, on fair moonlight nights,
Came mourning elves and gentle sprites,
Who, weeping much,
With tender touch
Soon hid her in the warm, sweet heather

POOR MARIONETTE

CONSIDER, NOW,
A PAINTER-MAN

ONSIDER, now, a painter-
man who thought him-
self divine,—
Correggio Delmonico del
Michael Angeline;
"Fine portrait-painting done
within," was printed on
his sign,
And all around his studio
his works hung on the
line.

When he painted little boys, he said: "How plainly I
can see,
I am such a mighty lion that they 're afraid of me!"
And when he painted little girls,—"Dear little things!"
said he,
"They 're shy because I awe them with my grace and
dignity."

22

" 'T is wonderful," he oft remarked, " the colors that I
know;
The sky is blue, the grass is green, and red the roses
blow;
And yet the people look amazed whene'er I paint them so,
And seem to think that higher yet an artist ought to go!"

Well, strange to say, it came to pass that he took down
the sign;
For never came a customer to buy his pictures fine.
And that is all I know of one who thought himself
divine,—
Correggio Delmonico del Michael Angeline.

NORTHERLY

WHEN the wind is east, they say,
We may have a rainy day;
When it travels from the west
Waving fields have little rest.
Warm and soft it is, we know,
When the southern breezes blow;
But this north wind puzzles me,—
Who knows *what* the weather 'll be!

A BALL 'S A BALL

A BALL 's a ball, and nothing more,
When it lies upon the floor.
See how grave and still its air!
Not a bit of frolic there.

What is this? Can Pussy's touch
Change the quiet thing so much?
See it start, and turn, and hop!
Pussy cannot make it stop!

See them scurry! See them leap!
See the two fall in a heap!
Now they roll! and now they run!
Bless me! balls are full of fun!

THE NAUGHTY LITTLE EGYPTIAN

Long, long ago, in Egypt land,
  Where the lazy lotus grew,
And the pyramids, though vast and grand,
  Were rather fresh and new,
There dwelt an honored family,
  Called Scarabéus Phlat,
Whose duty 't was all faithfully
  To tend The Sacred Cat.

They brought the water of the Nile
  To bathe its honored feet;
They gave it oil and camomile
  Whene'er it deigned to eat.
With gold and precious emeralds
  Its temple sparkled o'er,
And golden mats lay thick upon
  The consecrated floor.

And Scarabéus Phlat himself —
  A man of cheerful mood —
Held not his trust from love of pelf,
  For he was very good.

27

"EVER ON HIS BRONZÈD FACE HE WORE A LOOK OF GLEE."

He thought the Cat a catamount
In strength and majesty;
And ever on his bronzèd face
He wore a look of glee.

And Mrs. Scarabéus Phlat
Was smiling, bright, and good;
For she, too, loved The Sacred Cat,
As it was meet she should.
Never a grumpy syllable
Came from this joyous pair;
And all the neighbors envied them
Their very jolly air.

When Scarabéus went to find
The Sacred Cat its store,
The pretty wife he left behind
Stood smiling at the door.
He knew that quite as smilingly
She 'd welcome his return,
And brightly on the altar stone
The tended flame would burn.

The Sacred Cat was different quite;
No jollity he knew;
But, spoiled and petted day and night,
Only the crosser grew.
Yet still they served him faithfully,
And thought his snarling sweet;
And still they fed him lusciously,
And bathed his sacred feet.

So far, so good.   But hear the rest:
  This couple had a child,
A little boy, not of the best,—
  Rameses, he was styled.
This little boy was beautiful,
  But soon he grew to be
So like The Cat in manners,— oh!
  'T was wonderful to see!

He might have copied Papa Phlat,
  Or Mama Phlat, as well;
And why he did n't think of that
  No mortal soul could tell.
It was n't want of discipline,
  Nor lack of good advice,
But just because he did n't care
  To be the least bit nice.

Besides, he noticed day by day
  How ill The Cat behaved,
And how (whatever they might say)
  His parents were enslaved;
And how they worshiped silently
  The naughty Sacred Cat.
Said he, "They 'll do the same by me,
  If I but act like that."

At first the parents said: "How blest
  Are we, to find The Cat

Glow, humanized, within the breast
Of a Scarabéus Phlat!"
But soon the neighbors, pitying,
Whispered: " 'T is very sad!
There 's no mistake,— that little one
Of Phlat's is very bad!"

He snarled, he squalled from night till morn,
And scratched his mother's eyes,
The Sacred Cat, himself, looked on
In envious surprise.
And here the record suddenly
Breaks off. No more we know,
Excepting this: That happy pair
Soon wore a look of woe.

Yes, then, and ever afterward,
A look of pain they wore.
No more the wife stood smilingly
A-waiting at the door.
No more did Scarabéus Phlat
Display a jolly face;
But on his brow such sadness sat
It gloomied all the place.

So, children, take the lesson in,
And due attention give:
No matter when, or where, or how,
Mothers and fathers live,

No matter be they Brown or Jones,
  Or Scarabéus Phlat,
It grieves their hearts to see their child
  Act like a naughty cat.
And Sacred Cats are well enough
  To those who hold them so ;   .
But — oh, take warning of the boy
  In Egypt long ago!

SEEING IS BELIEVING

ILLING Kitty McHost was
deaf as a post,
And Wellington Stowe could
n't speak;
"So, you see, 't were as
well," said Miss Kitty
McHost,
"For a man to come courtin' in Greek!
If it 's me you are after, dear Wellington Stowe,
Just bring in a bit of a trumpet and blow."

So he blew and he blew, his dear lady to win;
But she cried in despair: "Will he never begin?"
And then in the trumpet he silently sighed,
Whilst fondly and sweetly his lady he eyed; —
"Would you deafen a body!" she cried, "Mr. Stowe;
If you blow loud as that, all the neighbors 'll know!"

And so it was settled. And long may they thrive,—
The quietest, happiest couple alive!

TELL ME, DAISY

TELL me, Daisy, ere I go,
Whether my love is true or no
One leaf off: He loves me.   What?
One more leaf, and he loves me not.
Three leaves: Will he?   Four leaves: So,
He never will love me? — oh no, no!
I don't care what a daisy says;
I 'm *sure* to get married one of these days!

AN OCEAN NOTION

WERE I old Neptune's son, you'd see
How soon the waves would bow to me;
And how the fish would gather round,
And wag their tails with joy profound.
I'd bid the sea-gull tidings bring
Of sunny lands where linnets sing;
I'd roam the icebergs wild, and find
A summer suited to my mind;
Or in the gulf-stream warm I'd play
And on my Nautilus sail away;
I'd turn the billows inside out;
Play leap-frog with the waterspout;
Swing on the cable, out of sight,
Or leap with dolphins to the light.
All this I'd do and more beside,
Were I old Neptune's joy and pride.
His wreathèd horn I'd lightly blow,
And swing his trident to and fro; .

And when I tired of ocean's roar,
I 'd take a little turn on shore.
If Neptune feared to trust on land

"AND ON MY NAUTILUS SAIL AWAY."

His fine aquatic four-in-hand,—
Why, what of that? I 'd laugh and go
Upon a charger sure and slow —

My turtle-steed so fine and grand
Ready for trip on sea or land.
Ah, but I'd have right lordly fun,
If I were only Neptune's son!

ARAMANTHA MEHITABEL BROWN

OH, Miss Aramantha Mehitabel Brown
Was known as the prettiest girl in the town,
    In the days of King George, number Three.
        Her hat was a wonder
        Of feathers and bows;
        The pretty face under
        Was sweet as a rose;
And her sleeves were so full they could tickle her
        nose!
        Her dimity gown was a marvel to see;
        So short in the waist!
        And not a bit laced—
"Oh, mercy! I never would do it!" said she.
No cumbering train hid her dear little feet,
Yet the skirt that revealed them was ample and
        neat,—
Indeed all the modistes declared it was "sweet";
And the bag that she swung from her plump little
        arm
Held a kerchief, a purse, and a luck-penny charm.

Ah, the maiden was fair,
And dainty and rare!
And the neighbors would sigh,
As she tripped lightly by:
"Sure, the pride of our town
And its fittest renown
Is sweet Aramantha Mehitabel Brown!"

"I CANNOT THINK WHAT KEEPS HIM SO."

COMING HOME

"COME, Kitty, come!" I said :
But still she waited — waited,
Nodding oft her pretty head
    With, "I 'm coming soon.
Father 's rowing home, I know,
I cannot think what keeps him so,
Unless he 's just belated;
    I 'm coming soon."

"Come, Kate!" her mother called,
"The supper 's almost ready."
But Kitty, in her place installed,
    Said, "I 'm coming soon.
Do let me wait. He 's sure to come;
By this time Father 's always home —
He rows so fast and steady;
    I 'm coming soon."

41

"Come, Kit!" her brothers cried;
But Kitty by the water
Still eagerly the distance eyed,
    With "I 'm coming soon.
Why, what would evening be," said she,
"Without dear father home to tea?
Without his 'Ho, my daughter'?
    I 'm coming soon."

"Come, dear!" plead one and all,
But Kitty 's softly humming;
She hears a cheery distant call,—
    "And he 's coming soon"
Is in her heart; for, far from shore,
Gliding the happy waters o'er,
She sees the boat, and cries, "He 's coming!
    We 're coming soon!"

THE witches hide in my books,
  I know,
Or else it 's fairy elves;
For when I study, they plague
    me so
  I feel like one of themselves.
Often they whisper: " Come and
    play,
  The sun is shining bright!"
And when I fling the book away
  They flutter with delight.
They dance among the stupid words,
  And twist the "rules" awry;
And fly across the page like birds,
  Though I can't see them fly.
They twitch my feet, they blur my eyes,
  They make me drowsy, too;
In fact, the more a fellow tries
  To study, the worse they do.
They can't be heard, they can't be seen —
  I know not how they look —
And yet they always lurk between
  The leaves of a lesson-book.
Whatever they are I cannot tell,
  But this is plain as day:
I 'll never be able to study well,
  Till the book-elves go away.

FANS

My sister Kitty has lovely fans,—
Oh, ten times finer than sister Nan's!
Kitty's are beautiful — satin and pearl
(Kitty was always a dressy girl!)
Ebony, tortoise-shell, lace, and gold;
Shimmering, shining in every fold;
Bedecked and trimmed with fur and feather,—
And she needs them even in winter weather!

Nan's (ah, how many she has!) are plain,
Clean, and cool as the summer rain;
Paper and palm-leaf fans are they,
Three for a dime, I have heard her say;

Strong and firm, yet light to bear,
And laden with cool, refreshing air,
As bound on errands of help and pity,
She carries them through the scorching city.

To-day she is sitting by tiny beds
Cooling poor little, suffering heads;
Fanning lightly — softly — slow
Till the little ones far into dreamland go.

I often think of these different fans,
Kitty's, so lovely — and sister Nan's.

EASY EXPECTATIONS

V'RY little grape, dear, that clings unto a vine,
Expects some day to ripen its little drop of wine.
Ev'ry little girl, I think, expects in time to be
Exactly like her own mama—as grand and sweet and free.
Ev'ry little boy who has a pocket of his own,
Expects to be the biggest man the world has ever known.
Ev'ry little piggy-wig that makes its little wail,
Expects to be a great big pig with a very curly tail.
Ev'ry little fluffy chick, in downy yellow drest,
Expects some day to crow and strut, or cackle at its best.
Ev'ry little kitten pet, so tender and so nice,
Expects to be a grown-up cat, and live on rats and mice.
Ev'ry little baby-bird that peeps from out its nest,
Expects some day to cross the sky from glowing east to west.
Ev'ry hope I've mentioned here will bring its sure event,
Excepting something happens; dear, to hinder or prevent.

46

A NEW YEAR

ING, dong! ding, dong!
This old year will soon be gone,
But a new one 's coming on,—
Ding, dong! ding, dong!

Tell us, Year, before you go,—
Ding, dong! ding, dong!
Why at last you hurry so,
Though at first so very slow?
Ding, dong!
Can't you wait until we see
What the new year means to be?
Ding, dong! ding, dong!

I wish years would never change;
No one wants a year that 's strange.
Ding, dong! ding, dong!
Big folk say 't would never do,
None would live the past anew;
But I 'd like it,— would n't you?
Ding, dong! ding, dong!

Just the same? No, I must be
Better with each year, you see.
Old Year, don't you pity me?
Ding, dong! ding, dong!
Ding!

THE ELF AND THE SPIDER

PERCHED on a stool of the fairy style,
An elf-boy worked with a mischievous smile.
" That careless spider ! " said he, " to leave
His web unfinished ! But I can sew:
I 'll spin, or sew, or darn, or weave —
Whatever they call it — so none will know
That his spidership didn't complete it himself,
Or I 'm a very mistaken young elf."

Well, the wee sprite sewed, or wove, or spun,
Plying his brier and gossamer thread;
And, quick as a ripple, the web, all done,
Was softly swaying against his head
As he laughed and nodded in joyful pride.
      Ho! ho! it 's done!
      Ha! ha! what fun!
And then he felt himself slowly slide —
Slide and tumble — stool and all —
In the prettiest sort of a fairy fall!

Up he jumped, as light as air ;
But oh, what a sight,
What a sorry plight —

"PLYING HIS BRIER AND GOSSAMER THREAD."

4

The web was caught in his sunny hair!
When, *presto!* on sudden invisible track,
That horrible spider came lumbering back:
" WHO 'S BEEN AT MY WEB? WHAT HO! COME ON! "
And he knotted for fight,
The horrid fright!
But the elf was gone —
Poor, frightened fay!
Nothing was seen but a tattered sheen,
Trailing and shining upon the green.

But all that night, with dainty care,
An elf sat tugging away at his hair.
And 't is whispered in Elf-land to this day
That any spider under the sun
May go and leave his web undone,
With its filmy thread-end swinging free
Or tied to the tip of a distant tree,
With never a fear that elfin-men
Will meddle with spider-work again.

DANCING

Master Fitz-Eustace de Percival Jones
   Went dancing with Polly McLever;
And he asked her that night, in the sweetest of tones,
   To dance with him only,— forever.

"Indeed I will, Eustace de Percival Jones,"
   Said dear little Polly McLever.
So he whispered her softly: "Delay is for drones —
   Let 's take the step now, Love, if ever."

To-day they are gray, and their weary old bones
   Feel keenly each turn of the weather;
But dancing at heart still are Polly and Jones,
   As they tread to-day's measure together.

A DEAR LITTLE SCHEMER

THERE was a little daughter once, whose stockings
    were so small
That when the Christmas Eve came round they
    would n't do at all.
At least she said they would n't do, and so she tried
    another's,
And folding her wee stocking up, she slyly took her
    mother's.

"I 'll pin this big one here," she said,— then sat before
    the fire,
Watching the supple, dancing flames, and shadows
    darting by her,
Till silently she drifted off to that queer land, you
    know,
Of "Nowhere in particular," where sleepy children go.

She never knew the tumult rare that came upon the
    roof!
She never heard the patter of a single reindeer hoof;
She never knew how Some One came and looked his
    shrewd surprise
At the wee foot and the stocking — so different in
    size!

"THE WEE FOOT AND THE STOCKING — SO DIFFERENT IN SIZE!"

She only knew, when morning dawned, that she was
   safe in bed.
" It 's Christmas! Ho!" and merrily she raised her
   pretty head;
Then, wild with glee, she saw what "dear Old Santa
   Claus" had done,
And ran to tell the joyful news to each and every
   one:

"Mama! Papa! Please come and look! a lovely doll,
   and all!"
And "See how full the stocking is! Mine *would* have
   been too small.
I borrowed this for Santa Claus.   It is n't fair, you
   know,
To make him wait forever for a little girl to grow."

THE ROAD TO LEARNING

WISH I knew my letters well,
     So I might learn to read and spell;
     I'd find them on my pretty card,
     If they were not so very hard.

Now S is crooked — don't you see?
     And G is making mouths at me,
     And O is something like a ball,—
     It has n't any end at all.

And all the rest are — my! so queer!
They look like crooked sticks — oh dear!
Nurse counted six, and twenty more;
What *do* they have so many for?

THERE 'S A SHIP ON THE SEA

THERE 'S a ship on the sea. It is sailing to-night,
    Sailing to-night!
And father 's aboard, and the moon is all bright,
    Shining and bright!
Dear moon, he 'll be sailing for many a night —
    Sailing from mother and me.
Oh, follow the ship with your silvery light,
    As father sails over the sea!

MAKING IT SKIP

"I 'LL make it skip!"
Cried Harry, seizing a bit of stone.
And, in a trice, from our Harry's hand,
With scarce a dip,
Over the water it danced alone,
While we were watching it from the land—
Skip! skip! skip!

"I 'll make it skip!"
Now, somehow, that is our Harry's way:
He takes little troubles that vex one so,
Not worth a flip,
And makes them seem to frolic and play
Just by his way of making them go
Skip! skip! skip!

THE FANCY-DRESS BALL

They dressed me, one day, for a juvenile ball,
In a long-tailed coat and a *chapeau* tall,
And ruffles and bows and an eye-glass, too,
And a wig finished off with an odd little queue:
But what I was meant for I hardly knew.

"You belong to Directory days, my dear,"
They said, which struck me at least as queer,

For I knew that the mass of the people in town,
From De Lancy and Astor to Jenkins and Brown,
Were in the Directory all set down.

My sisters tried hard my attention to fix,—
I heard, "No, in France," and "In ninety-six,"
And "Turbulent days," and "Yes, there were five";
And each to out-rattle the other would strive—
They buzzed in my ear till I felt like a hive.

"Oh, is n't he perfect?" they cried in delight
(And, really, I was n't a very bad sight),
But every youngster, I 'll venture to say,
At the ball, whether peasant or clown or fay,
Had been praised at home in the selfsame way.

Well, all but me were as plain as your hat;
At once you could say, they are this or they 're that;
I even knew good little George with his hatchet,
(Without, I must own, any sapling to match it);
And you felt, at a glance, he expected to "catch it."

I recognized Tell by his high Swiss hat,
His boy with the apple a-top, and all that;
But all of the characters stared at me,
As if to say, "What on earth can *he* be?"
And what was the use of my saying, you see,
"Why, I? I am from the Directory!"

MORAL.

When you 're booked for a fancy-dress party, take care
To learn all about the queer costume you wear!

BILLY BUTTERCUP

Bonny Billy Buttercup! Pretty little fay.
Riding on the blossoms in the breeze;
Deep in the clover-bloom hiding him away,
Startled at the murmur of the trees.

Children! have you seen him? shy is he and gay,
Sunny as the butterflies and bees,
Bonny Billy Buttercup! Pretty little fay!
Riding on the blossoms in the breeze.

THE SWEET, RED ROSE

"Good morrow, little rose-bush!
Now prithee tell me true:
To be as sweet as a sweet, red rose
What must a body do?"

"To be as sweet as a sweet, red rose
A little girl like you
Just grows and grows and grows and grows—
And that's what she must do."

AN APRIL GIRL

The girl that is born on an April day
Has a right to be merry, lightsome, gay;
And that is the reason I dance and play
And frisk like a mote in a sunny ray,—
    Would n't you
    Do it, too,
If you had been born on an April day?

The girl that is born on an April day
Has also a right to cry, they say;
And so I sometimes *do* give way
When things get crooked or all astray,—
    Would n't you
    Do it, too,
If you had been born on an April day?

The girls of March love noise and fray;
And sweet as blossoms are girls of May;
But I belong to the time midway,—
And so I rejoice in a sunny spray
Of smiles and tears and hap-a-day,—
    Would n't you
    Do it, too,
If you had been born on an April day?

Heigh-ho! and hurrah! for an April day,
Its cloud, its sparkle, its skip and stay!
I mean to be happy whenever I may,
And cry when I must; for that 's my way.
Would n't you
Do it, too,
If you had been born on an April day?

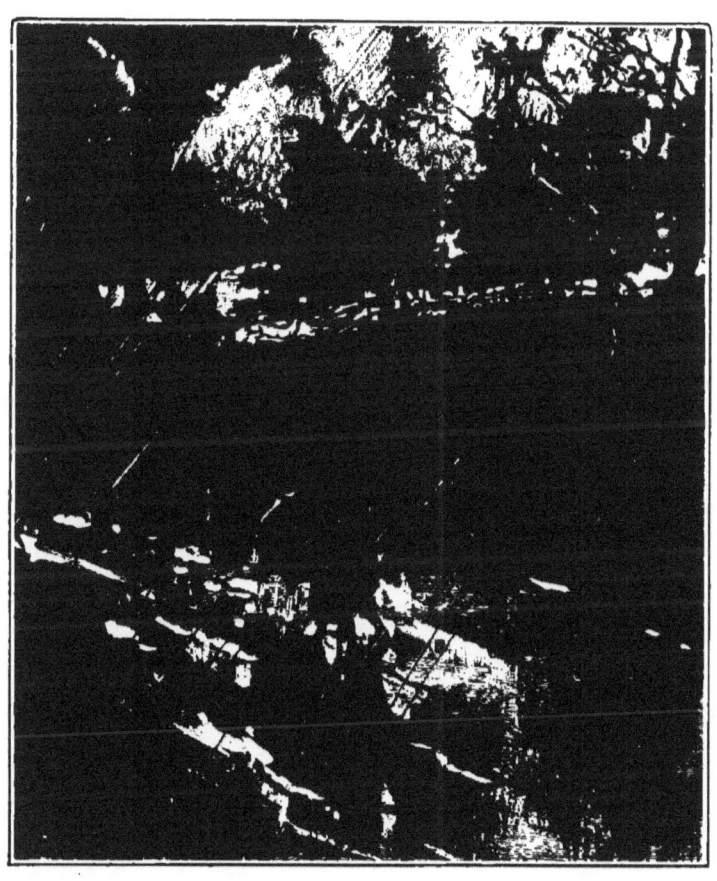

THE ZEALLESS XYLOGRAPHER

(Dedicated to the End of the Dictionary.)

A XYLOGRAPHER started to cross the sea
  By means of a Xanthic Xebec;
But, alas! he sighed for the Zuyder Zee,
  And feared he was in for a wreck.
He tried to smile, but all in vain,
Because of a Zygomatic pain;
And as for singing, his cheeriest tone
Reminded him of a Xylophone —
Or else, when the pain would sharper grow,
His notes were as keen as a Zuffolo.
And so, it is likely, he did not find
On board, Xenodochy to his mind.
The fare was poor, and he was sure
Xerophagy he could not endure;
Zoöphagous surely he was, I aver,
This dainty and starving Xylographer.
Xylophagous truly he could not be —
No sickly vegetarian he!
He'd have blubbered like any old Zeuglodon
Had Xerophthalmia not come on.
And the end of it was he never again
In a Xanthic Xebec went sailing the main.

THE LITTLE GIRL WHO TRIED TO MIND

PRUDENCE — good sister Prudence!—was a gentle girl
  of eight,
And Totty was but four years old, when what I now
  relate
Came to the happy little pair, one bright November
  day —
A Sunday, too — while good Papa was many miles
  away.

" Good-by, my darlings! don't forget." The little ones
  went forth,
Their hearts all in a sunny glow, their faces to the
  north —
Their faces to the chilling north, but not a whit cared
  they,
Though the pretty church before them stood full
  half a mile away.

For Mother, with her smiling face and cheery voice,
  had said :
" I cannot go to church to-day, but you may go instead.
Baby will need me here at home — the precious little
  pet !
But babies grow in time, you know. She 'll go to
  meeting yet."

66

"Take care of sister, Prue!" she said, while tying
    Totty's hood,—
"And, Tottykins, I 'm sure you 'll be, oh, *very* still and
    good!
Good-by, my darlings! Don't forget. Prudence, you
    know the pew;
And, Tot, be Mama's little mouse, and sit up close to
    Prue."

In truth it was a pretty sight, to see the rosy pair
Walk down the aisle and take their seats, with sweetly
    solemn air.
And Prudence soon was listening, her manner all
    intent,
While little Tot sat prim and stiff, and wondered
    what it meant.

The quaint, old-fashioned meeting-house had pew-
    seats low and bare,
With backs that reached above the heads when they
    were bowed in prayer.
And thus it was when suddenly a squeaking sound
    was heard,
Faint at the first, then almost loud — even the deacon
    stirred!

All heads were bowed; again it came — that tiny
    puzzling sound,
The staidest members rolled their eyes and tried to
    look around;
Till Prudence, anxious little maid! felt, with a pang
    of fear,
That, whatsoe'er its cause might be, the noise was
    strangely near.

Out went her slyly warning hand, to reach for Totty
    there;
When, oh, the squeaking rose above the closing words
    of prayer!

An empty mitten on the seat was all that Prudence
 felt,
While on the floor, in wondrous style, the earnest
 Totty knelt!

Poor Prudence leaned and signaled, and beckoned,
 all in vain; —
Totty was very much engaged and would not heed,
 't was plain.
When suddenly a childish voice rang through the
 crowded house: —
"DON'T, Prudy! 'cause I 've dot to be my Mama's 'ittle
 mouse!"

Many a worshiper looked shocked, and many smiled
 outright,
While others mourned in sympathy with "Prudy's"
 sorry plight;
And Totty, wild with wrath because she could be
 mouse no more,
Was carried soon, a sobbing child, out through the
 wide church-door.

———

Now parents ponder while ye may upon this sad
 mishap;
The mother, not the mouse, you see, was caught
 within the trap.
And when your little listening ones you send beyond
 your reach,
Be chary of your metaphors and figurative speech.

5 *

THE FAIR-MINDED MEN WHO WALKED
TO DONAHAN

Two wise men walked to Donahan
    Upon a rainy day,—
        Heigh-ho!
With one umbrell' between them.
They hit upon an honest plan
    For both to have fair play,—
        Heigh-ho!
I wish you could have seen them.

Said one: "I'll hold it half the way,
    And you the other half,—
        Heigh-ho!
And safely we'll go skipping."
But soon his neighbor said: "Nay, nay,
    You're dry, and have your laugh,—
        Heigh-ho!
While I catch all the dripping.

"Now *this* we'll try: Your head poke through,
    And I will do the same,—
        Heigh-ho!
There! nothing could be better;

Now one umbrell' will serve for two,
    And neither 'll be to blame,—
        Heigh-ho!
If t' other gets the wetter."

And so they walked to Donahan,
    Nor found the journey long,—
        Heigh-ho!
Until they fell a-wheezing;
"The bargain 's honest, man to man,"
    They said; "but something 's wrong,"
        Heigh-ho!
As on they went — a-sneezing.

A BROWN-STUDY.

A BROWN STUDY

MOTHER said: "That 's all, dear. Now run outdoors and
    play."
            Father said the same;
            And so I came.
But, somehow, they forget that I 'm growing every day.

A girl can't *always* frolic. Why, lambs are sometimes
    still,
Though whenever they feel like it, they caper with a
    will.
And birds may stop their singing while their hearts are
    full of song.
I 've seen them look so solemn! And when the day is
    long
They often hide among the boughs and think,— I 'm
    sure they do;
I 've peered between the twitching leaves, and seen
    them at it, too!

But if a girl stands still and thinks, the people always
    say:
" As you 've nothing else to do, dear, why don't you go
    and play?"

Well, all I know is this: It 's nice
To jump the rope, and skip and swing, or skate on
　　winter ice;
It 's nice to romp with other girls and laugh as well
　　as they,—
　　　　　But not to-day.

Dear me! How sweet and bright it is, this lovely,
　　lovely Earth!
And not a thing upon it dreams how much it 's really
　　worth.
Except the folks.　They calculate and set themselves
　　quite high;
　　　　　Oh, my!

You dear, good sky, to bend so soft and kind above
　　us all!
It 's queer to think this great wide world is nothing
　　but a ball
　　　　　Rolling, they say, through space;—
　　　　　(How *does* it keep its place?
None of my business, I suppose.)—I wonder if the
　　brook
Is full to-day.　It 's early yet;—I guess I 'll go and
　　look.

"A MISS IS AS GOOD AS A MILE"

"A Miss is as good as a mile" I think
  When pretty Kitty Lee
Leaning upon the well's soft brink
  Lingers to talk with me
And mother wonders why I don't
  Get home in time for tea.

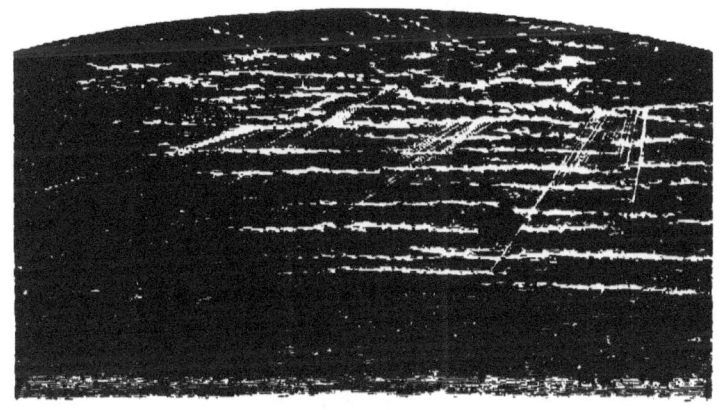

"O BIRD of the sky,
How far you can fly,—
And all in a minute!
You 've been to the sky,
Away up so high,
And know all that 's in it;
You 've pierced with your flight
Its wonderful light —
What makes it so blue?
Now tell me, oh do,
Little singer!"

The bird stopped a while
To rest on a stile,
With mosses upon it;

And ere very long,
He poured forth a song
  As sweet as a sonnet.
But never a word
My waiting ear heard,
  Why the sky was so blue,
  Though he told all he knew —
    Stupid singer!

I went in to look
For the facts in a book,
  All told to a letter;
Yet somehow it seemed
(Though maybe I dreamed)
  The bird told it better.
Oh, never a word
My willing ear heard,
  Why the sky was so blue,
  Yet he told me quite true
    Knowing singer!

MY DOG

I LOVE my dog — a beautiful dog,
  Brave and alert for a race;
Ready to frolic with baby or man;
  Dignified, too, in his place.

I like his bark,— a resonant bark,
  Musical, honest and deep;
And his swirling tail and his shaggy coat
  And his sudden, powerful leap.

Never a smug little pug for me,
  Nor a Spitz with treacherous snap!
Never a trembling, pattering hound,
  Nor a poodle to live on my lap!

No soft-lined basket for bed has Jack,
  Nor bib, nor luxurious plate;
But our open door, that he guards so well,
  And the lawn are his royal state.

No dainty leading-ribbon of silk
  My grand, good dog shall fret;
No golden collar needs he to show
  He's a very expensive pet;

But just my loving voice for a chain,
   His bound at my slightest sign,
And the faith when we look in each other's eyes
   Proclaim that my dog is mine.

He never was carried in arms like a babe,
   Nor dragged like a toy, all a-curl;
For he proudly knows he 's a dog, does Jack,—
   And I 'm not that sort of a girl.

I KNOW A LITTLE MAIDEN

· I KNOW a little maiden who
can knit and who can
sew;
Who can tuck her little
petticoat, and tie a
pretty bow;
She can give the thirsty
window-plants a cool-
ing drink each day,
And dust the pretty sit-
ting-room, and drive
the flies away.
She can bring Papa his dressing-gown, and warm his
slippers well,
And lay the plates and knives and forks, and ring the
supper-bell;
She can learn her lessons carefully, and say them with
a smile,
Then put away her books and slate and atlas, in a
pile;

She can feed the bright canary, and put water in his
    cage ;
And soothe her little brother when he flies into a rage.
She can dress and tend her dollies like a mother, day
    or night,—
Indeed, one half the good she does I cannot now recite.
And yet there are some things, I 'm told, this maiden
    cannot do.
She cannot say an ugly word, or one that is not true;—
Who *can* this little maiden be ? I wonder if it 's you.

A NEW SONG TO
AN OLD TUNE ·

"You are old, my dear deacon," the schoolma'am re-
marked,
"And studies with youth pass
away;
Yet you 're quite in ad-
vance of the books, I am
sure,—
Now tell me the reason, I
pray."

"In the days of my youth,"
the good deacon replied,
"I was fleetest of foot in
my set;
And I ran on ahead of my
studies so fast
That they 've never caught
up with me yet."

THERE once was a man with a sneeze,
Who always would sit in a breeze.
    When begged to take shelter
    He 'd cry: "I should swelter!"
And straightway go on with his sneeze.

INTERNATIONAL

SHE came from a round black dot on the map,—
This dear little girl, and she's called a Jap.
Maybe my sister will show it to you:—
The very place where this little girl grew.

I wish she knew some American words,
Such as "How do you do?" and "trees," and "birds."
I 'd like to talk with her ever so much —
But she can't tell a thing that I say from Dutch.

Well, our dollies will get us acquainted to-day
If she 'll only come out in the Park to play!
If it were not for nodding, and taking their hands,
We could never know people from foreign lands.

SURPRISE

WHAT was the moon a-spying
Out of her half-shut eye?
One of her stars went flying
Across the broad blue sky.

MOTHER

EARLY one summer morning,
  I saw two children pass;
Their footsteps, as they loitered,
  Wakened the dewy grass.

One, lately out of babyhood,
  Looked up with eager eyes;
The other watched her wistfully,
  Oppressed with smothered sighs.

" See, Mother ! " cried the little one,
  " I gathered them for you —
Clover and pretty buttercups!
  And Mabel has some too."

" Hush, Nelly ! " whispered Mabel,
  " We have not reached it, yet.
Wait till we get there, darling,
  It is n't far, my pet."

" Get where ? " asked Nelly.   " Tell me."
  " To the churchyard," Mabel said.
" No! no ! " cried little Nelly,
  And shook her sunny head.

Still Mabel whispered sadly,
  " We must take them to the grave.

Come, darling !" and the childish voice
    Tried to be clear and brave.

But Nelly still kept calling
    Far up into the blue;
" See, Mother, see, how pretty!
    We gathered them for you." ·

And when her sister pleaded,
    She cried — and would not go : —
" Angels don't live in graveyards;
    My mother don't, I know ! "

Then Mabel bent and kissed her.
    ' So be it, dear," she said;
" We 'll take them to the arbor
    And lay them there instead.

" For mother loved it dearly,
    It was the sweetest place ! "
And the joy that came to Nelly
    Shone up in Mabel's face.

I saw them turn and follow
    A path with blossoms bright,
Until the nodding branches
    Concealed them from my sight;

But still like sweetest music
    The words came ringing through :
" See, Mother, see, how pretty!
    We gathered them for you."

"PHILOPENA!"

THE pretty Princess Wilhelmina
Thought she 'd eat a Philopena.
She asked the Prince. He answered "Yea";
And "caught" was he that very day.
The present came in course of time;
No jewel it, nor gold nor delf.
The Prince just waited for his prime,
Then gave the Princess fair — himself!

CONFUSION

HEIGH-HO! I 've left my "B O, bo,"
And "A B, ab"—oh, long ago!
    And gone to letters three.
(Dear me! What *does* that last word spell —
The last I learned? I knew it well —
    It 's W and E and B.)

You see, I 've so much work to do —
Scrubbing and sweeping, dusting too —
    I can't remember half I know.
And oh! the spiders drive me wild,
Till Mother says: "What ails the child?
    What makes her fidget so?"
(Now, sakes alive! What can it be —
That W and E and B?)

As soon as school is out, I run
To do my work. It 's never done,
    But when my lesson once is said
    It goes and pops out of my head —
All on account of dust and dirt.
No matter how my hands may hurt,
    I sweep and toil the livelong day,
    And try to brush the things away.

(It 's all the spiders — don't you see?)
And yet I 'm glad I 've learned to spell.
(What *is* that word? I knew it well —
That W and E and B!)

PUZZLED FAIRY-FOLK

On one sole eve of the bright, long year
There is trouble in Fairy-land;
There is dread, and wonder, and elfin fear
At something they never can understand.

For "Why?" says the Queen,
And "Why?" say the elves,
And "What does it mean?"
They ask of themselves.
"We 'd like to know why,
On the Fourth of July,
These mortals make such a commotion?
Rattle and flash! Fountains of fire
Play low, play round, play higher and higher;
Now, what it 's about,
This terrible rout,
We have n't the ghost of a notion."

Poor little fairy-folk, dear little sprites!
What can you know of wrongs and of rights,
Battles and victories; birth of a nation?
Heed not these jubilant echoes of fights; —
Dance and rejoice in your lightsome creation.

"THERE IS TROUBLE IN FAIRY-LAND."

MILD FARMER JONES AND THE NAUGHTY BOY

"COME DOWN FROM OUT MY HICKORY-TREE."   "YOU WON'T, YOU NAUGHTY BOY? OH FIE!"

CRIED Farmer Jones, "What 's this I see?
Come down from out my hickory-tree!
Come down, my boy; I think you might;
To steal is neither wise nor right."

"You won't, you naughty boy? Oh, fie!
You dare to tell me mind my eye?

HIS FAITHFUL DOG HAS MOUNTED GUARD.   "MY STROKES SHALL BRING DOWN TREE AND ALL."

Come down this instant! What d' you say?
'Takes two to make a bargain,'— eh?"

Now, Farmer Jones, as mild a man
As any, since the world began,
Resolves on action fierce and bold,—
Although it makes his blood run cold.

His faithful dog has mounted guard;
There is an ax in yonder yard,—
"Now, though the heavens quake and fall,
My strokes shall bring down tree and all!"

Fast come the blows, but vain the plot;
The tree may yield, the boy will not.
His pelting nuts the farmer blind;
Yet still the ax its cleft doth find.

Ah! who is this doth cry "Hold up!
I say, tie fast that yelping pup;
Do the square thing by me, and see
If I don't leave your hickory-tree?"

'T is done. The faithful dog is tied,
The shining ax is turned aside.

THE TREE MAY YIELD, THE BOY WILL NOT   "I SAY, TIE FAST THAT YELPING PUP."

"NO HOAXING, NOW?" THE YOUTH DOTH CRY.   SAID JONES, "YOU 'RE SORRY NOW, I SEE."

"No hoaxing, now?" the youth doth cry —
And Farmer Jones replies, "Not I."

Now, mingling with the song of bird,
A sound of tearing clothes is heard,
And scraping boots; and, with a bound,
That naughty boy stands on the ground.

Said Jones, "You 're sorry now, I see,
For knocking nuts from off my tree!"
"Well, yes; if you 'll just hold the pup,
And let a fellow pick 'em up."

7

"All right! my boy," cried Farmer Jones,
Who felt delighted in his bones;
For never since the world began
Was seen so very mild a man.

ALARMED

A VERY nervous elephant
One day became afraid
That he was growing rather fat.
"Dear me!" said he, "if I thought *that,*
I should at once be weighed!"

WHAT HAPPENED TO NELLY

I KNEW a little girl,—
  You? Oh, no,—
Who came to live on earth,
  Just to grow;
Just to grow up big
  Like Mama,
"Big as any lady,"
  Said Papa;
Not to stay a baby
  As she came;—
Yet each morning found her
  Quite the same.

Quite the same, they said,
  Not a change
Since she went to bed—
  Ah, how strange!
Baby Nell at night,
  Baby Nell at dawn,

Everything the same,
Not a dimple gone.
They saw her every hour,
So you 'll own,

BABY NELL.

If a change had come,
They 'd have known.

Yet the clothes grew small —
Sleeves and frocks;
She could n't wear her bibs,
Nor her socks.

7·

Soon she stood alone
　Yes, indeed! and walked!
Then she toddled round;—
　Then she talked!

Then she tried to help,
　All she could;
Busy little mite,
　Kind and good!
Well, as years went on,—
　Seven, maybe,—
Not a soul could call
　Nell a baby.

"THEN SHE TODDLED ROUND."

Still Mama declared,
  Every minute
She had been the same—
  What *was* in it?

She saw her all the time,
  So you 'll own,
If a change had happened
  She 'd have known.
Baby Nell herself,
  Though uncommon wise,
Ne'er had seen an inch
  Added to her size.
Even Pomp, the dog,
  Never seemed to say:
"Nell is not the same
  Now as yesterday."

Yet, as I have said,
  Clothes kept growing small,
Tight at first, and then
  Would n't do at all.
Even Nelly's toys,
  Skipping-rope and hoop,
Once quite big enough,
  Now would make her stoop.
Why, her very crib
  Seemed to shrink away,
Till it cramped the child
  Any way she lay.

So, from hour to hour,
  Not a person knew,
Looking straight at Nell,
  That she ever grew.
Little baby Nell,
  On the nurse's knee,
Little Nell at school
  Learning A B C.

Then — ah, it was quick!
  Came the reading class;
Then arithmetic, —
  Clever little lass!

How *did* it happen?
When *did* she change?
No one had noticed —
Was n't it strange!

Show me when a bud
Changes to a rose,
Then I 'll tell you truly
When a baby grows.

THE SECRET

I WATCHED a butterfly on the wing; .
I saw him alight on a sunny spray.
    His pinions quivered;
    The blossoms shivered;
I know he whispered some startling thing.
    But why so bold,
    Or what he told,
While poising there on the sunny spray,
I 've never learned to this blessed day.

THISTLES!

THREE velvety, busy, buzzing bees
Once plunged in a thistle-plant up to their knees.
Alas! Though plucky and stout of heart,
They bounded away with an angry start.
For the thistle 's the touchiest thing that grows;
It 's the crossest old plant! as every one knows.
And now they 'll give you a bit of advice:
"Don't ever run into a thistle-plant twice!"

THISTLES !

JEANNETTE AND JO.

JEANNETTE AND JO

Two girls I know—Jeannette and Jo,
  And one is always moping;
The other lassie, come what may,
  Is ever bravely hoping.

Beauty of face and girlish grace
  Are theirs for joy or sorrow;
Jeannette takes brightly every day,
  And Jo dreads each to-morrow.

One early morn they watched the dawn —
  I saw them stand together;
Their whole day's sport, 't was very plain,
  Depended on the weather.

" 'T will storm!" cried Jo. Jeannette spoke low;
  "Yes, but 't will soon be over."
And, as she spoke, the sudden shower
  Came, beating down the clover.

"I told you so!" cried angry Jo;
  "It always *is* a-raining!"

Then hid her face in dire despair,
Lamenting and complaining.

But sweet Jeannette, quite hopeful yet,—
I tell it to her honor,—
Looked up and waited till the sun
Came streaming in upon her;

The broken clouds sailed off in crowds,
Across a sea of glory.
Jeannette and Jo ran, laughing, in—
Which ends my simple story.

———

Joy is divine. Come storm, come shine,
The hopeful are the gladdest;
And doubt and dread, dear girls, believe,
Of all things are the saddest.

In morning's light, let youth be bright;
Take in the sunshine tender;
Then, at the close, shall life's decline
Be full of sunset-splendor.

And ye who fret, try, like Jeannette,
To shun all weak complaining;
And not, like Jo, cry out too soon—
"It always *is* a-raining!"

Down in the meadow, close by the hill,
 Some one is having a party;
Never was heard on a summer night still,
 Buzz of enjoyment so hearty.

Strange! for the elves are no longer on earth.
 Strange! for the fairies are over!
But, sure as you live, there are frolic and mirth
 For somebody, down in the clover.

LITTLE SQUIRRELS, CRACK YOUR NUTS

LITTLE squirrels, crack your nuts;
Chirp your busy tune;
Sound your merry rut-a-tuts —
Boys are coming soon!
Hide to-day, and pile to-day,
Hoard a goodly store;
When the boys are gone away,
You may find no more.
Hear you not their merry shout,
Song, and happy laughter?
Sure as leaping, boys are out!
Girls are coming after.
Hide and pile, then, while you may;
Hoard a goodly store;
If the children come this way,
You may find no more.

"Old King Cole was a jolly old soul,
 And a jolly old soul was he;
He called for his pipe, and he called for his bowl,
 And he called for his fiddlers three."

Now who were the fiddlers? And what did they fiddle,
 And where were the fiddlers three?
A fiddle for fiddles! King Cole is a riddle—
 The fiddlers are down by the sea.

I

Two dear friends sat down to tea;
And both were sleek and fair to see.

II

All went well until one spied
Great danger near. "Oh, look!" she cried.

114

III

A furious, uninvited beast
Was rushing madly to the feast.

IV

Quick as a flash they trapped the foe,
Then tied him fast, and bade him "Go!"

V

Then safely from a tall tree near
They saw him madly disappear.

VI

Departed foe! Delighted friends!
And so this thrilling story ends.

THE SAD STORY OF LITTLE JANE

A Calendar of Woe.

Jan — e, little saint, was sick and faint,
Feb — rifuge she had none;
Mar — malade seemed to make her worse,
Apr — icots were all gone.
May — be, she thought, in some fair field,
June — berries sweet may grow;
July — and June, they searched in vain,
Aug — menting all her woe.
Sept — imus failed to find a pill —
Oct — oroon slave was he;
Nov — ice, poor thing! at feeling ill,
Dec — eased ere long was she.

MOTHER'S ARM

FROM the low, wide, sheltering wall
Baby drops his pretty ball;
Baby wants it, that is all.

Why should mother hinder so,
Why not let the baby go?
Baby's wish is law, you know.

'T will not always be the way;
Baby 'll go alone some day.
Mother cannot always stay,—
Well-a-day.

A SUGGESTION FOR A HAPPY NEW YEAR

SUPPOSE we think little about number one;
Suppose we all help some one else to have fun;
Suppose we ne'er speak of the faults of a friend;
Suppose we are ready our own to amend;
Suppose we laugh with, and not at, other folk,
And never hurt any one "just for the joke";
Suppose we hide trouble, and show only cheer —
'T is likely we 'll have quite a Happy New Year!

UNSETTLED

I 've a sailor suit; and a boat to row;—
And yet there 's something I 'd like to know:

If I am a stupid (as some folks agree),
Why then it is plain that a stupid I be.
But if I 'm no stupid, then clever am I,
And likely I 'll be quite a chap, by and by.

120

TWINKLE, twinkle, little star—
I don't wonder what you are!
I've learned more of you, you see,
Than you'll ever know of me.

THE LETTERS AT SCHOOL

ONE day the letters rushed to school,
  And hindered one another;
They got so mixed 't was really hard
  To pick out one from t' other.

A went in first, and Z came last;
  The rest were all between them,—
K, L and M, and N, O, P,—
  I wish you could have seen them!

B, C, D, E and J, K, L
  Soon jostled well their betters;
Q, R, S, T — I grieve to say —
  Were very naughty letters.

Of course, ere long they came to words —
  What else could be expected?
Till E made D, J, C and T
  Decidedly dejected.

But, through it all, the Consonants
  Were rudest and uncouthest,
While all the pretty Vowel girls
  Were certainly the smoothest.

And simple U kept far from Q,
  With face demure and moral,

"Because," she said, "we are, we two,
  So apt to start a quarrel!"

But spiteful P said, "Pooh for U!"
  (Which made her feel quite bitter),
And, calling O, L, E to help,
  He really tried to hit her.

Cried A, "Now E and C, come here!
  If both will aid a minute,
Good P will join in making peace,
  Or else the mischief 's in it."

And smiling E, the ready sprite,
  Said, "Yes, and count me double."
This done, sweet peace shone o'er the scene,
  And gone was all the trouble!

Meanwhile, when U and P made up,
  The Cons'nants looked about them,
And joined the Vowels; for, you see,
  They could n't do without them.

FOUR LITTLE BIRDS

Four little birds all flew from their nest,—
Flew north, flew south, flew east and west;
They thought they would like a wider view,
So they spread their wings and away they flew.

DRESSING MARY ANN

I

SHE came to me one Christmas day,
In paper, with a card to say:

II

"*From Santa Claus and Uncle John,*"—
And not a stitch the child had on!

III

"I 'll dress you; never mind!" said I,
."And brush your hair; now, don't you cry."

IV

First, I made her little hose,
And shaped them nicely at the toes.

V

Then I bought a pair of shoes,—
A lovely "dolly's number twos."

VI

Next I made a petticoat;
And put a chain around her throat.

VII

Then, when she shivered, I made
  haste,
And cut her out an underwaist.

VIII

Next I made a pretty dress;
It took me 'most a week, I guess.

IX

And then I named her Mary Ann,
And gave the dear a pretty fan.

X

Next I made a velvet sacque
That fitted finely in the back.

XI

Soon I trimmed a lovely hat,—
How pleased and sweet she looked in that!

XII

O, I forgot, that was n't all,
I bought her next a parasol!

She looked so grand when she was dressed,
You really never would have guessed
How very plain she seemed to be,
The day when first she came to me.

THE FROG, THE CRAB AND THE LIMPSY EEL

A FROG, a crab and a limpsy eel
  Agreed to run a race.
The frog leaped so far he lost his way.
  And tumbled on his face.
The crab went well, but quite forgot
  To go ahead as he went,
And so crawled backward every step —
  On winning the race intent.
And the limpsy eel, he curled and curled,
  And waved to left and right,
Till the crab came backing the other way,
  And the frog jumped past them quite.
But when last I looked, the limpsy eel
  Was curling himself apace,
The frog had tangled his two hind legs,
  And the crab had won the race!

NEW-YEAR'S DAY

" A HAPPY New Year to you, my lady!
To give you this greeting I came."
" Oh, thank you, indeed," said the sweet little lady,
" And, truly, I wish you the same."

" I wish you many returns, my lady,
A long chain of years, I may say,

Linked into garlands of joy, my lady,
And now I must bid you good day."

"Yes, many returns," said the bright little lady,
"In sooth, I would wish for them, too;
A long, long chain," said the dear little lady,
"Of beautiful visits from you!"

TO A YOUNG GIRL

With a Spray of Autumn Leaves.

THOUGH autumn winds be sighing in your future,
    Molly dear,
Their music may be sweeter than the early spring-
    time cheer;
As the fleeting moments ripen in the fullness of your
    prime,
There 'll be tints and shadows richer far than those of
    summer-time;
And, so, these leaves prophetic made me dream, my
    girl, of you,
As they trembled in their gladness, with the sunlight
    shining through.

9*

CAT'S-CRADLE

" IT 's criss-cross high, and it 's criss-cross flat;
Then four straight lines for the pussy cat;
Then criss-cross under; ah, now there 'll be
A nice deep cradle, dear Grandpa! See!

" Now change again, and it 's flat once more —
A lattice-window! But where 's the door?
Why, change once more, and, holding it so,
We can have a very good door, you know.

" Now over, now under, now pull it tight;
See-saw, Grandpa! — exactly right!"
So prattled the little one, Grandfather's pet,
As deftly she wrought. "See, now it 's a net!

" But where did you learn cat's-cradle so well?"
She suddenly asked; and he could not tell.
He could not tell, for his heart was sore,
As he gravely said, "I have played it before."

What could the sweet little maiden know
Of beautiful summers long ago?
Of the merry sports, and the games he played,
When "Mama," herself, was a little maid?

What could she know of the thoughts that ran
Through the weary brain of the world-worn man ?
But she knew, when she kissed him, dear Grandpa
  smiled,
And that was enough for the happy child.

SIGNS OF MAY

MAY day and June day,
  Spring and summer weather,
Going to rain; going to clear;
  Trying both together.
Flowers are coming! No, they 're not,
  Whilst the air 's so chilly;
First it 's cold, then it 's hot —
  Is n't weather silly?

S'pose the little vi'lets think
　Spring is rather funny.
So they hide themselves away,
　Even where it 's sunny.
S'pose the trees must think it 's time
　To begin their growing.
See the little swelling buds!
　See how plain they 're showing!
S'pose they know they 're going to make
　Peaches, apples, cherries.
Even vines and bushes know
　When to start their berries.
Only little girls like me
　Don't know all about it:
Maybe, though, the reason is
　We can do without it.
Winter-time and summer-time
　We keep on a-growing;
So, you see, we need n't be—
　Like the flowers, and like the trees,
　And the birds and bumblebees—
Always wise and knowing.

JOHNNY AND MEG

"STRAWBERRIES! Ripe strawberries!"
Cried lusty Johnny Strong;
And he sold his baskets readily
To folks who came along.

But soon a tiny voice piped forth,
"Me, too!" Meg could not shout
As John did. Yet she too must sell
The fruit she bore about.

"Ho, STRAW-BERR-E-E-S!" roared lusty John,
"Me, too!" piped Meg, so sad.
Now Johnny made good sales that day,
But Meg sold all she had.

ON THE LAGOON

(Jackson Park, Chicago, 1893.)

"FULL!" cried the gondolier. *Swish!*—and they started.
Great was the crowd, but they would not be parted;
So in they all scrambled—from Clara to Kitty—
Little white citizens of the White City.

THE PENSIVE CRICKET

ONE cold November morning,
All kind companions scorning,
A pensive cricket sought
In melancholy thought
His woes to stifle.
"Alas! alas!" cried he,—
"Ah woe, ah woe is me!
I really do not see
Why I should be
So melan — melancholy.
Ah me!
Let 's see."

He thought, and thought, and thought,—
That cricket did.
"It is not love, nor care,
That fills me with despair.
My chirp is sharp and sweet,
And nimble are my feet;
My appetite is good,
And bountiful my food;
My coat is smooth and bright;
My wings are free and light,—

Then ah, and oh, ah me!
What can the matter be ? ”

Long time the cricket sighed,
And muttered low: “ Confound it ! ”
Then joyfully he cried:
“ Eureka! Oh, Eureka ! ”
By which he meant, “ I 've found it ”—
The learned little shrieker!
“ It is — ah, well-a-day !
Because my girl 's away,
My nimble, dimble Dolly,
My cheery, deary Polly.
Oh, Queen of little girls ! —
I like her sunny curls;
I like her eyes and hair,
Her funny little stare,—
Her way of jumping quick
Whene'er she hears me click.
She 's loving and she 's neat,
She 's spry and true and sweet;
And though I caper free,
She never steps on me.
Kee-nick! kee-nick!
Ker-tick ! a-tick !
And now the thought has come,—
To-morrow she 'll be home!
My Polly, Polly, Polly,
My nimble, dimble Dolly!

I 'll dance to-night
In the bright moonlight,
To-morrow I 'll see Polly! —
Tra la! How very jolly!"

———

Next night the house with pleasure rang,
For Polly-girl had come;
The cricket on the hearthstone sang,—
And home once more was home.

˙ POOR JACK-IN-THE-BOX

FRIGHTEN the children, do I? Pop with too sudden a
 jump?
Well, how do you think I felt, all shut in there in a
 lump?
And did n't *I* get a shock when the lid came down on
 my head?
And if *you* were squeezed up and locked in, would n't
 you get ugly and red?
If you think I 'm so dreadful, my friend, suppose you
 just try it yourself;
Let some one shut *you* in a box, and put you away
 on the shelf —
And then, when the lid is unhooked, if *you* don't leap
 out with a whack,
And look like a fright when you spring, I 'll give in,
 or my name is n't Jack.

WHY

ONCE I was a little maid
  With eager heart and mind;
And through the wondrous hours, I sought
  Something I could not find.

No single thing; 't was that, to-day,
  To-morrow, it was this;
And wistfully I heard folk say:
  "A funny little miss!

"She queries so! She wonders so!"
  They said —"the pretty thing!"
But what I sought, or wished to know,
  They quite forgot to bring.

And now that I am older grown,
  And do as I 've a mind,
When little lips ask, "Why?"—I 'll own
  To answer I 'm inclined.

Their "How?" and "What?" and "Why?" you see,
  Mean that they, too, would reach
And find a something that they need
  In some one's friendly speech.

SUNNY DAYS

DID you ever go on sunny days
The pretty flowers to pull,
And, kneeling in the meadow,
Fill your little apron full?
Did you ever see the daisies shine,
And hear the robins start,
Till you sometimes found it hard to tell
The flowers and song apart?
Did you ever see a butterfly
Upon the blossoms sway,
And leave it free to rest unharmed,
Or go its fluttering way?
And did you ever feel the breeze
Steal lightly to your cheek,
As if it loved you very much
And had a word to speak?
Well, if you have known all these things
So beautiful and wild,
I'm sure the birds and flowers and breeze
Have known a happy child.

ALICE IN WONDERLAND

SWEET Alice, while in Wonderland,
  Found a fine baby-brother;
She took him by his little hand,
  And said: "We 'll look for Mother."

And soon they met a dolphinet,
  Twice in a single day;
Said she: "How queer! You 're waiting yet!
  Why don't you go away?"
"Because," said he, "my ways are set,
  And who are you, I pray?"

I think I 'm Alice, sir," said she,
" But Alice had no brother;
I can't quite make it out, you see,
    Until I find my mother."

Then, low, the dolphinet replied,
" 'T is passing strange," said he,—
That mother, on my cousin's side,
    Is next of kin to me!"

And so they journeyed far and wide,
    A family of three; —
And never on a single point
    Did one of them agree!

TO W. F. C.

(*With a Copy of "Alice's Adventures in Wonderland"*)

TAKE a nibble from the book
　At its rightest side.
Down and down the rabbit hole
　Let your fancy slide;
In a whiff you 'll be so small,
You 'll not know yourself at all;
　Ah, 't will be delicious joy—
　Just to be a little boy!

Take another nibble then—
　At the left side, not the wrong—
And beyond the ranks of men
　Up you 'll stretch, sir, tall and strong!
You will find your very own
　In the land where you belong;
Yet be like a bubble blown
　Over realms of fun and song.
Light as thistle-down you 'll float;
　Firm as granite you will stand;
Sailing in a paper boat
　Fast and far through Wonderland!

THE LITTLE BIG WOMAN AND THE BIG LITTLE GIRL

A LITTLE big woman and a big little girl,
  They merrily danced all the day;
The woman declared she was too small to work;
And the girl said: "I'm too big to play."
    So they merrily danced
      While the sunlight stayed,

And practised their steps
In the evening shade.

"We must eat," said the little big woman.   "Why not?"
"Why not?" said the big little girl;
So when supper-time came, they sipped as they skipped,
And swallowed their cake in a whirl.
And they merrily danced
While the twilight stayed,
And practised their steps
In the evening shade.

NANNY ANN

"Oh, Nanny Ann! the sun is bright,
The sky is blue and clear;
All ugly clouds are out of sight,
No rain to-day, my dear.
No need, as I can plainly tell,
For you to take your fine umbrell'.
Go to the spring, my pretty daughter;
Fetch me a jug of sparkling water."

Now Nanny Ann herself was bright;
  Says she: "Though skies are clear,
And ugly clouds are not in sight,
  'T is April, mother dear.
The ways above, no soul can tell;
I 'd rather take my fine umbrell'."
So saying, off she went for water; —
Now was not she a wise young daughter?

THE FOUR LITTLE IMPS

FOUR little imps and four little birds
  Lived up in the selfsame tree;
And the kindly ways of those four little imps
  Were a beautiful sight to see.

They fed and tended those orphan birds
  All through the blossoming days;
And never were tired of sitting around
  And watching their comical ways.

Their pitiful squeak they took for a song
  As sweet as they ever had heard;
And they sometimes laughed, and oftener sighed,
  In feeding each motherless bird.

So, gently they tended them, day by day,
  Till their four little pets had grown
And longing to go to the beautiful sky,
  Each bird from the nest had flown.

And when all were gone, the four little imps
  Did wipe their eight little eyes,
And scamper away to assuage their grief —
  Which seems to me rather wise.

THE SMILING DOLLY

I whispered to my Dolly,
    And told her not to tell
(She 's a really lovely Dolly —
    Her name is Rosabel).

" Rosy," I said, " stop smiling,
    For I 've been dreadful bad;
You must n't look so pleasant,
    When I am feeling sad!

"I took Mama's new ear-ring,—
　　I did, now, Rosabel,—
And I never even asked her,—
　　Now, Rosy, don't you tell!

"You see I 'll try to find it
　　Before I let her know;
She 'd feel so very sorry
　　To think I 'd acted so."

Still Rosabel kept smiling;
　　And I just cried and cried —
And while I searched all over,
　　Her eyes were opened wide.

"Oh, Rosy, where I dropped it
　　I can't imagine, dear";
And still she kept on smiling,—
　　I thought it very queer.

I had wheeled her round the garden
　　In her gig till I was lame;
Yet when I told my troubles,
　　She smiled on, just the same!

Her hair hung down her shoulders
　　Like silk, all made of gold,
I kissed her, then I shook her,
　　Oh, dear! how I did scold!

"You 're really naughty, Rosy,
　　To look so when I cry;

When *my* mama 's in trouble
I never laugh,—not I."

And *still* she kept on smiling,
    The queer, provoking child!
I shook her well and told her
    Her conduct drove me wild.

When — only think ! that ear-ring
    Fell out of Rosy's hair !
When I had dressed the darling,
    I must have dropped it there.

She doubled when I saw it,
    And almost hit her head!
Again I whispered softly,
    And this is what I said:

" You precious, precious Rosy !
    Now I 'll go tell Mama
How bad I was — and sorry —
    And oh, how good you are !

" For, Rose, I had n't lost it —
    You knew it all the while,
You knew I 'd shake it out, dear,
    And that 's what made you smile."

How do birds first learn to sing?

From the whistling wind so fleet,
From the waving of the wheat,
From the rustling of the leaves,
From the raindrop on the eaves,
From the children's laughter sweet,
From the plash when brooklets meet.

Little birds begin their trill
As they gaily float at will
In the gladness of the sky,
When the clouds are white and high;
In the beauty of the day
Speeding on their sunny way,
Light of heart, and fleet of wing —
That's how birds first learn to sing.

LITTLE NORWAY SPRUCE.

CHRISTMAS EVE

ALL night long the pine-trees wait,
Dark heads bowed in solemn state,
Wondering what may be the fate
        Of Little Norway Spruce.

Did they take him for his good? —
Gallant little tree that stood
Only lately in the wood —
        Little Norway Spruce!

Gone the pretty tree so trim,
Lithe was he, and strong of limb!
All the pines were proud of him,—
      Little Norway Spruce.

That night the lonely little tree
In the dark stood patiently,
Far away from forest free,
      Little Norway Spruce.

Chained and laden, but intent
On the pines his thoughts were bent;
They might tell him what it meant,
      Little Norway Spruce!

Morning came. The children. "See!
Oh, our glorious Christmas-tree!"
Gifts for every one had he; —
      Happy Norway Spruce!

THE CIRCUS CLOWN'S DREAM

A CIRCUS CLOWN dreamed a
   dream, one night,
     That wakened him with
      laughing;
And when he told it in high
   delight,
     Of how he dreamed of a
     circus horse
     That flew through the air
     as a matter of course,
     His comrades thought he
     was chaffing.

"Not so," he declared. "I say
   it is true";
     And they opened their eyes with
     wonder.
"I saw him as plain as I now see you;
     That horse swung, too, on a high
     trapeze,—
     And he lifted me up from my hands and knees
     Till gaily I swung under.

"He slid down the pole like a half-ton cat,
   And swung by a rope, my cronies.
Then he vaulted and climbed like an acrobat;

He lay on his back, spun a ball with his feet,—
And his spring-board leaping was quite complete:
Why, he leaped over three fat ponies!

" What 's more, he did the aquarium act,
    Stayed under water among the fishes!
  You need n't wink,— it 's a solemn fact.
    Then as ' the Great Professor Equine
    And his Wonderful Sons,' O friends of mine!
    He exceeded my proudest wishes.

" But that was n't all of my wondrous dream,—
    So full of magic and clatter.
  You should have heard the spectators scream
    When three great lions, with grace and ease,
    Began to juggle like Japanese
    With stick and ball and platter.

"Then my turn came," said the circus clown,
  "For I had to earn my money;
So I ambled up, and nimbled down,
  And gave my liveliest tricks and jokes,—

11*

I was doing my best to amuse the folks,—
As funniest of the funny,—

"When all the people burst out crying,
And begged me hard to stop my trying.
In vain I gave my comical blink
And changed my costumes, quick as a wink;
You never heard such wails and weeping.
This put a sudden end to my sleeping;
I 'woke to learn, though strange it may seem,
They wept because 't was the end of my dream!"

AN APPEAL

BY UNCLE JOHN

OH, children, if you love us,—
Heed well this pleading song!
When we bid you learn your lessons,
Don't study them too long.

And, children, since ingratitude
The meanest is of crimes,
When we give you drums and trumpets,
Won't you play on them sometimes?

When, now and then, we offer you
Fresh caramels, oh, pray,—
We do beseech you, darlings,—
Don't throw them all away.

And don't be greedy, either,
With Dr. Allopath,
But try to be content, when ill,
With all the drugs he hath.

Enough's enough. Yet little ones
This riddle pray unlock:
Why *do* you go to bed so soon
And give us such a shock,
Instead of saying: "Well, this once
We'll wait till ten o'clock"?

ROBBY'S SPAN.

ROBBY'S SPAN

In the soft, green light of the leafy June,
"Maud S." and "Nancy" were humming a tune;
Humming and chatting, they soberly swayed
In the hammock under the linden's shade.

Said "Maud S." to "Nancy": "To make them quite
    strong,
  Mama said we scarcely could take too much pains";
"Oh, yes!" answered "Nancy," "and ever so long! —
  But, how funny for horses to make their own reins!"

A live pair of horses. They worked side by side,
As each a crochet-needle daintily plied.
Their true names were Polly and Alice Adair,
And never was seen a more beautiful pair.

Spirited, supple, strong, gentle, and fleet
  Were "Maud S." and "Nancy," as Robby allowed,
Rob was their master, — so chubby and sweet.
  And surely he had a good right to be proud.

Such a grip as he had! Such a "*whoa!*" and a "*go!*"
Such a power over horses—(of *their* kind, you know);
Such a genius for making them follow his will,—
For speeding them madly, or holding them still!

Well, it seems that one day, when the spirited span
   Were hitched to a rose-bush that stood by the door,
At the sight of a spider, they broke loose and ran;
   And Robby sat wailing as never before.

His lines were all tangled, and broken, and torn.
The rose-bush rained petals, and sprang back in scorn,
For "Maud S." and "Nancy," as Robby declared,
"Had turned into girls just because they were scared!"

In vain they begged pardon, flushed, laughing and
   warm;
   In vain coaxed and kissed in their prettiest style;
But at last, by a promise, they conquered the storm,
   And won from their master a nod and a smile.

They would make him "a new set of reins—good
   and strong!"
Make him "reins that were nearly a dozen yards
   long!"
Ah, "Maud S." and "Nancy"—you beautiful span!
'T is you who can manage the stout little man!

And this was the reason they swung side by side,
As each a crochet-needle daintily plied; —
Their true names were Polly and Alice Adair,
And never was seen a more beautiful pair.

HIS REPORT

THERE was a worthy schoolmaster
Who wrote to the trustees

A full report, three times
a year, in words quite
like to these:
"The scholars are so
orderly, so studious
and kind,
'T is evident I have a
gift to train the youth-
ful mind."

172

EIGHT-DAY CLOCKS

(A Rhyme for Young Calculators)

How often I 've sustained a shock,
Since I have owned my eight-day clock!
At first, I wound it once a week,
(Bless me! how the key did creak!)
And then I pondered, " Where 's the need?
The thing would go at even speed
A whole day longer, if neglected;
And I, for one, can't be expected
To wind and wind on every Sunday
A clock that 's bound to run till Monday."
And yet each week to add a day,
And recollect, is not my way;
And this it is that bothers me; —
My clock and I do not agree.

Suppose *you* buy an eight-day clock,
And add it to your household stock,
And wind it every week, we 'll say,
Heeding not that extra day;
How many times (to be quite clear)
Must it be wound within the year?
And on the other hand suppose
You let it run till toward its close,

And so, on each eighth day, delight
In winding it with gentle might,
And never miss the task — 't is clear,
You 'll wind it fewer times a year;
But just how many times, you see,
May best be told by *you*, not me.

TINSEL WITHOUT, BUT METAL WITHIN

I 'M only my lady's page—
　And just for the night of the ball—
To prance on a parlor stage,
　And run at her beck and call.

I 'm only my lady's page,
　But mark me, my fellows, all
You 'll be civiler men, I 'll engage,
　When I pommel you—after the ball.

BERRY-TIME

FLOWERS and fruits of the summer,
  Can you hear us children shout,
When, over the fields and hillsides,
  We seek and find you out?

Do you hide from us ever on purpose,
  And, deep in the green, keep still?
Or is it quite social and pleasant
  When basket and pail we fill?

And the bumblebees — how can you bear them?
  Well, sometimes, I think it is true
They have their sharp stings for us people,
  And only their velvet for you.

IN BLACKBERRY SEASON.

12

THE THREE TIGERS

THREE tigers went to take a drink;
And what do you think? What *do* you think?
They drank as much as heart could wish,
And never swallowed a single fish.

A TERRIBLE TIGER

A TIGER who signs himself T
Is a gourmand most dreadful to see;
He eats and he eats
All possible meats,
And all kinds of sweets,
Then fears that they will not agree.

FAR AWAY

ONE night, in the bright, warm summer,
  Mother went — oh, so far away!
So very far! Yet quite near her,
  In my pretty bed I lay.

She stood and looked from the window,
  In the moonlight cool and clear;
I called her as she stood there,
  But mother did not hear. . . .

She did not hear when I called her —
  She was gone so very far!
I lay and wished I was only
  The moonlight, or a star;

Then she might soon have known it —
  How lonely I was for her.
But I waited, and waited, and waited,
  And mother did not stir.

180

At last she turned, and smiling
  Said, "You awake, little Jack?"
But I only could sob and kiss her —
  So glad that mother was back!

HANS CHRISTIAN ANDERSEN

(Copenhagen, August 4, 1875)

THERE is silence in the Northland, for one hath passed
   away
Honored of all, a poet-soul, weary for many a day —
Weary of earth, of suffering, of toil and cumbering care,
Eager to lay the burden down, but willing still to bear.
A silence in the Northland. For Denmark's heart is
   sad —
Sad for the gentle Andersen, the youngest soul she had!

Sad for the countless little ones who crowd about his
    bier,
Glad for the voice that evermore the listening world
    shall hear!

There is joy among the angels.   To that bright company
One cometh as a little child — all gladly cometh he!
Our Lord hath lifted off his load, hath led him to the
    light,
And happy spirits, welcoming, lead up the pathway
    bright.
Now shall the ransomed poet hear the choir of perfect
    song,
The grand, eternal story he hath waited for so long!
O children! ye for whom he wrought his lore of magic
    sway,
In grateful thought still honor him the Lord hath called
    this day!

TROUBLED

If it were not for fairies, this world would be drear;
  (I 'm sure they are true,— heigh-ho !)
    The grass would not tangle,
    The bluebells would jangle,
The days would be stupid and queer, you know,
And everything dull if the fairies should go.
  (I 'm sure they are true,— heigh-ho !)

I love to believe in the godmother's mice,
    And Hop-o'-my-Thumb, heigh-ho !
    And it 's cruel in Willy
    To call me a silly.
If brothers would only be nice, you know,
Not tease and make fun, all my troubles would go,—
I 'd believe in the fairies forever,— heigh-ho !

THE FARMER WHO BECAME DRUM-MAJOR

Peggy and Meggy tell the story in their own way.

Peggy : OUR father worked upon a farm,
      He wore a linen smock;
Meggy : 'T was gathered to a yoke on top,
      And hung down like a frock.

Peggy : Oh, he was very meek,
      And mother used to scold him,
Meggy : And he would always do
      Exactly what we told him,—
Peggy :   *Ex-actly* what we told him.

Meggy : His shoulders had a little stoop
　　　　Which mother tried to cure :
Peggy : She used to say his shambling walk
　　　　She scarcely could endure.

Meggy : But he played the fiddle well,
　　　　And sang on Sunday sweetly;
Peggy : He beat the time for all,
　　　　And knew the tune completely,—
Meggy :   Yes, knew the tune com-*pletely.*

Peggy : When mother called, "Come, John!"
　　　　he came,
　　　　And smiling chopped the wood;
Meggy : He drew the water, swept the path,
　　　　And helped her all he could.

Peggy : He used to romp with Meg and me,
Meggy :   Yes, and with Polly Wentels,
Peggy : But oh, my sakes! That was before
　　　　He put on regimentals!
Meggy :   Yes, put on regimentals!

Peggy : For, oh, a big militia-man,
　　　　One evening after tea,
Meggy : Came in and coaxed our father dear
　　　　To join his company.

Peggy : For men were very scarce
　　　　That summer in our village,

Meggy :   And so they all prepared
                They said for war and pillage.
Peggy :   Just think! for war and pillage!

Meggy : Well, after that he dropt the smock,
                He stood up stiff and straight;
Peggy : And when we called for wood and things,
                We always had to wait.

Meggy : Still, he was rather meek,
                And mother still could scold him;
Peggy : He nearly always did
                Exactly what we told him,—
Meggy :   *Ex-actly* what we told him.

Peggy : But soon he had a big mustache,
                He stalked about the farm;
Meggy : He went to drill three times a week,
                And could n't see the harm.

Peggy : At last he told our mother
                A thing that did enrage her.
Meggy : "*Rid-dic-u-lus!*" she said,
                " For you to be *drum-major!* "
Peggy :   For *him* to be drum-major!

Meggy : He wore a splendid soldier coat,
                He bore a mighty staff;
Peggy : But oh, he lost his gentle ways,
                And would n't let us laugh.

Meggy : He grew so very fierce
           He soon began to scold us,
Peggy : And then *we* had to do
           Exactly what *he* told us!
Meggy :   *Ex-actly* what he told us!

Peggy : We used to run and hide away —
Meggy :   *You* did — not *I*, dear Peg!
Peggy : Why, yes, you often did it, too,
           Now don't deny it, Meg!

Meggy : He scared us 'most to death,
           He walked just like a lion;
Peggy : And when he coughed out loud
           He set us both a-cryin'!
Meggy :   Yes, set us *both* a-cryin'!

Peggy : He would n't play, he would n't work,
         The weeds grew rank and tall;
Meggy : The pumpkins died; we did n't have
         Thanksgiving Day at all.

Peggy : The farm is spoiled. It is n't worth,
         Ma says, a tinker's wager.
Meggy : Now, was n't it a dreadful thing
         For him to turn drum-major ?
Both :   A savage, awful, stark, and stiff
         Ridiculous drum-major!

COURTESY

A PRETTY little boy and a pretty little girl
 Found a pretty little blossom by the way;
Said the pretty little boy to the pretty little girl:
"Take it, O my pretty one, I pray!"

Said the pretty little girl to the pretty little boy:
"I must hold my Sunday bonnet, sir, you see;
So, I thank you very kindly, but I'd very much
 prefer
 You should carry it, and walk along with me."

MAY BLOSSOMS

"Good morrow!" Spring said to us all,
When boisterous winds were blowing;
But now it's "Good day!" for it's May —
And never a morrow can come this way
More fair and blithe than a day in May,
Or brighter than this that is going.

Now is she not lovely and true?
And is she not wise and knowing?
If it were not for her, why, what would they do —
The things that are ready for growing?
So good day to us all! for it's May,
And never a morrow can come this way
More tender and fair than a sweet May day,
Whatever way she be going.

EIGHT GOOD THINGS ABOUT DOBBIN

DOBBIN never would do us harm,
Dobbin takes us over the farm;
Dobbin follows us when we call;
Dobbin never will let us fall.
Dobbin is white as the whitest snow,—
Dobbin shows even at night, you know.
Dobbin is patient, steady, and kind;
Dobbin can teach us children to mind.
　　Whether it 's "Whoa! Dobbin,
　　　Dear old Dobbin,"
　　Or "Go! Dobbin,
　　　Dear old Dobbin,"
Dobbin will mind, as a matter of course;
But everybody can't be a horse.
　　Hey, Dobbin！

SIDE BY SIDE

"What is the little one thinking about?
Very wonderful things, no doubt."

WHAT are the old folks thinking about?
Very wonderful things, no doubt.
A thought like this filled the baby's head
(A wonderful baby, and very well bred).
He gazed at grandpa, and grandma too;
And mirrored the pair in his eyes of blue,
As side by side they sat there, rocking —
He with his pipe, and she with her stocking.

And the baby wondered, as well he might,
Why old folks always were happy and bright —
And he said in his heart
With a blithe little start
That showed how gladly he 'd act his part:
"I 'll find some baby, as soon as I can,
To stay with me till I 'm grown an old man,
And, side by side, *we 'll* sit there, rocking —
I with my pipe, and she with her stocking."

A SMART BOY

I 'M glad I have a good-sized slate,
With lots of room to calculate.
Bring on your sums! I 'm ready now.
My slate is clean; and I know how.
But please don't ask me to *subtract*,
I like to have my slate well packed;
And only two long rows, you know,
Make such a miserable show;
And, please, don't bring me sums to *add*;
Well, *multiplying* 's just as bad;
And, no, I 'd rather not *divide* —
Bring me something I have n't tried!

195

SEVEN LITTLE PUSSY-CATS

SEVEN little pussy-cats, invited out to tea,
 Cried: "Mother, let us go. Oh, do! for good
  we 'll surely be.
 We 'll wear our bibs and hold our things as
  you have shown us how—
 Spoons in right paws, cups in left—and make
  a pretty bow;
We 'll always say, 'Yes, if you please,' and 'Only half
 of that.'"
"Then go, my darling children," said the happy Mother
 Cat.

The seven little pussy-cats went out that night to tea,
Their heads were smooth and glossy, their tails were
 swinging free;

They held their things as they had learned, and tried
to be polite;—

With snowy bibs beneath their chins they were a
pretty sight.

But, alas for manners beautiful, and coats as soft as
silk!

The moment that the little kits were asked to take
some milk

They dropped their spoons, forgot to bow, and — oh,
what do you think?

They put their noses in the cups and all began to
drink!

Yes, every naughty little kit set up a " me-ouw!" for
more,

Then knocked the tea-cup over, and scampered through
the door.

S. DAVIS.

"ELEVEN SHYLY PICKED THE BONES OF 'LEVEN BITS OF FISH."

ELEVEN LITTLE PUSSY-CATS

Eleven little pussy-cats invited out to dine.
Eleven little bowls they found, all waiting in a line;
Eleven little me-ows they gave, eleven little purrs,
Eleven little sneezes, too, though bundled in their furs,
Eleven, after soup was served, stood close around a dish,
Eleven shyly picked the bones of 'leven bits of fish.
Eleven courses, I am told, composed this rare repast,
Eleven bits of catnip, too, when cream came on at last;
Eleven times they licked their paws when all the cream
    was out,
Eleven times they bobbed their heads and said 't was
    so, no doubt.
Eleven times they thought they heard the squeaking of
    a mouse.
Eleven times apologized to the lady of the house;
Eleven softly purred, " Good-by; we 've had a lovely
    time ! "
Eleven scampered home again. So ends this simple
    rhyme.

JACK AND JILL

LONG, long ago, a Mother said
  Unto her children small:
"Now Jack and Jill, go up the hill—
  And see that you don't fall.
Fetch me a pail of water back,
  And hurry with a will."
"Oh, no, mama," said lazy Jack.
  "Oh, yes, mama," said Jill.

The Mother frowned an angry frown;
  They went as she directed—
Alas, she saw them coming down
  Sooner than she expected!
You know the story, children all?—
  If Jack had scorned to grumble,
Perhaps he 'd not have had that fall,
  And made his sister tumble.

IN HASTE

SAID a Turtle: "Pray pardon my haste;
I have n't a moment to waste;
Do you see that big sign
Where the gentlemen dine?
Do you note that it mentions to-day?
When my head is well out
I know what I 'm about;—
My motto is HASTE AND AWAY!"

SOAP-BUBBLES

FILL the pipe!
  Gently blow;
Now you 'll see
  The bubbles grow!
Strong at first,
  Then they burst,
And then they go
  To nothing, O!

THE PAMPERED POODLE

THERE was once a little poodle, who so lost his self-
respect,
That his honest tail refused to do his wagging.
"For in truth"—the tail continued—"I cannot but
object
To the petting he submits to, and the nagging.

" I scorn to wag for any dog who cannot gnaw a bone
 Without whining for a nurse to come and chop it,
And who sits all day, be-ribboned, like a puppet on a
 throne,
And I 'll never wag again if he don't stop it.

" What with bibs, and bows, and baskets, and mummery
 forlorn,
And laziness, and nonsense, he 's a noodle!
And, now you know my reasons, can you wonder that
 I scorn
To wag for so ridiculous a poodle?"

MASTER THEODORE

(Old Nurse's Story.)

ITTLEBAT Titmouse Theodore
Van Horn
Was the prettiest baby that ever was
   born.
I bathed him and fed him and taught
   him " Bo-peep,"
Rocked him and trotted him, sang
   him to sleep.
Then I bade him good-by, and crossed the wide sea,
And it rolled twenty years 'twixt that baby and me;
Till at last I resolved I would cross the blue main
And hug my own precious wee baby again.

Well, that old ship creaked, and that old ship tossed,—
I was sure as I lived that we all should be lost,—
But at last we saw sea-gulls, and soon we saw land;
And then we were in; and — if there did n't stand
My own blessed baby! He came there to meet me!
Yes, when we all landed, he hastened to greet me!

And wonder of wonders! that baby had grown
To be bigger than I, and he stood all alone!

"Why, Nursey!" he said (he could talk, think of that!),
As he bowed like a marquis and lifted his hat.
"Ah, how *did* you know your old Nursey? Oh, my!
You 've changed very much, and no wonder," says I;
When I spied of a sudden his mother, behind,—
Sweet lady! She 'd helped him his Nursey to find.
And he told me, right there, he 'd a sweet little wife
And I should live with them the rest of my life.

So I 'm here, and right happy. You just ought to see
The dear little fellow who sits on my knee.
He has beautiful dimples and eyes like Mama,
And his nose and his chin make you think of Papa.
Ah, me! He 's a beauty! There never *was* born
A lovelier babe than this latest Van Horn.

FORBIDDEN

"KEEP off the Grass!" the sign-board said;
  And children turned away,
Wondering sadly why the grass
  Objected to their play.

The Summer sped; in time the snow
  In circling flurries came,
And hid the grass, although the board
  Protested still the same.

"Keep off the Grass!" 'T was plain as day;
  And birds who came along,
Pausing in wonder, cocked their heads,
  And hushed their chirpy song.

"What's that? what does it mean?" they asked;
  And one bird twittered low:
"The Summer must be buried here;
  Oh, comrades, let us go!"

TEN LITTLE DOLLS

TEN pretty little dolls are we
As happy as the day,
Black and white, short and tall,
Grave and grand and gay;
Ten pretty dolls all waiting here,—
Who will come and play?
Come and take us, little maidens,
Ere we run away.

JACK'S WISH

IF a pretty fairy should come to me,
And ask: "What thing would you like to be?"
  I 'd say: "On the whole,
  I will be a mole."
Oh, that would be just the thing for me!
  I 'd go straight down, and not care a fig
What squirming things in the ground I 'd meet;
  For if I were a mole, I 'd dig and dig
Till my nose should tickle the Chinamen's feet!

A DUTCH FAMILY

'ERE 's all our leetle vamily —
Myzelf and zisters two.
Big Rychie's eyes don't open vide,
And leetle Katzie's do.

Katzie 's zo zlow and plump-y!
And Rychie 's grown zo tall!
But all the zense she has n't got
You vood not miss at all.

Ve 'd be a vunny vamily
If it vos not for me;
For I 'm the only boy ve have,
And zmartest of the three.

212

LITTLE MISS KITTY

Dear little Miss Kitty
Was going to the city,
And feared she might be late;
So she called to a man:
"Oh, sir, if you can,
Please tell those cars to wait!"

"THE WORTHY POOR"

A DOG of morals, firm and sure,
Went out to seek the "worthy poor."
"Dear things!" she said, "I 'll find them out,
And end their woes, without a doubt."

She wandered east, she wandered west,
And many dogs her vision blest,—
Some well-to-do, some grand indeed,
And some—ah! very much in need.

So poor they were!—without a bone,
Battered and footsore, sad and lone;
No friends, no help. "What lives they 've led,
To come to this!" our doggie said.

"I should not give to them; I 'm sure
They cannot be the worthy poor.
They must have fought or been disgraced;
My charity must be well placed."

Some dogs she found quite to her mind;
So thrifty they—so sleek and kind!
"Ah me!" she said, "were they in need,
To help them would be joy indeed."

'T was still the same, day in, day out,—
The poorest dogs were poor no doubt;
But they were neither clean nor wise,
As she could see with half her eyes.

'T is strange what faults come out to view
When folks are poor. She said: "'T is true
They need some help; but as for me,
I must not waste my charity."

So home she went, and dropped a tear,
"I 've done my duty, that is clear.
I 've searched and searched the village round,
And not one 'worthy poor' I 've found."

And all this while, the sick and lame
And hungry suffered all the same.
They were not pleasant, were not neat —
But she had more than she could eat!

O ye who have enough to spare!
To suffering give your ready care;
Waste not your charitable mood
Only in sifting out the good.

For, on the whole, though it is right
To keep the "worthy poor" in sight,
This world would run with scarce a hitch
If all the rich were the worthy rich.

JINGLE

A BLACK-NOSED kitten will slumber all the day;
A white-nosed kitten is ever glad to play;
A yellow-nosed kitten will answer to your call;
And a gray-nosed kitten I would n't have at all!

AFTER TEA

YES, somewhere, far off on the ocean,
  A lover is sailing to me;
A beautiful lover! Nurse found him
  One night in my cup, after tea.

Whenever the cruel wind whistles,
  I think of that ship on the sea,
And tremble with terror lest something
  May happen, quite dreadful to me.

And then, when the moon rises softly,
  I hardly can sleep, for, you see,

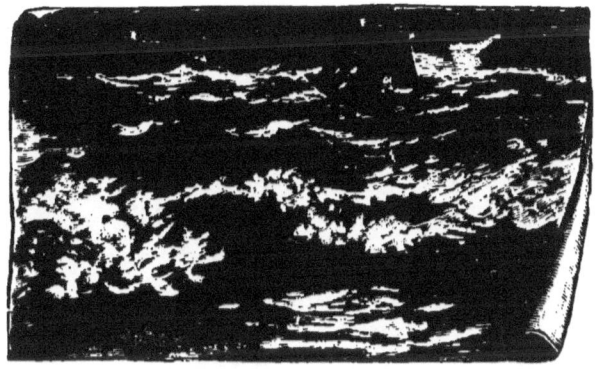

I know that its beautiful splendor
Is lighting my lover to me.

But oh, if he *should* come! Why, Nursey,
I 'd hide like a mouse. Deary me!
What nonsense it is! But you should n't
Be finding such things in my tea.

THE SPRINT RUNNER

"LEARNING? What's the use of learning?"
Johnny cried, his lesson spurning.
"As for me, I'd rather run!"
So, from morn to set of sun,
Johnny's legs were never still;
He could distance Bob and Bill,
Jim, and Tom, and Dick, and Peter,
Not a youth in town was fleeter.

Grammar, algebra, and history
Glimmered in a hazy mystery,
School terms softly sped away,
While he sprinted day by day,—
Week by week, and through vacation.
Then his friends in desperation,
Vowed the boy was not for knowledge,
So they sent him off to college.

FUN AT GRANDMAMA'S

ONE Christmas day at Grandmama's, we all dressed up,
    for fun;
And sat in a line and called them in to look when we
    were done.
We never laughed a single time, but sat in a solemn
    row.
Tommy was Queen Elizabeth, and Jane wore an Alsace
    bow.
Freddy was bound to be a nun (though he did n't look
    it a bit!)
And Katy made a Welsh-woman's hat and sat down
    under it.
Sister was Madame de Maintenon, or some such Frenchy
    dame;
And Jack had a Roman toga on, and took a classic name.
As for poor me, I really think I came out best of all,
Though I had n't a thing for dressing up, 'cept Dinah's
    bonnet and shawl.
Well, Grandma laughed, and Grandpa laughed, and all
    admired the show,—
I wish I 'd seen us sitting there, so solemn, in a row!

THE KNOWING LITTLE FISH

"Ahem! now we are ready!" said a knowing city chap,
  As he flung his hook, well baited, and heard it strike
    "kerflap!"
"This cloudy day is just the one; the game is sure to
    bite.
  I 'll have a jolly basketful to show the folks, by night."

And "Ha! ha! ha!" laughed the happy little fish,
" Now we are safe and cozy as any one could wish!
For we know about that funny thing that lives upon
    the land,
And we 're not the fools he takes us for, he 'll please
    to understand."

THE BEES THAT WENT TO THE SKY

Fuzzy Wuzz, Buzzy Wuzz, Zipperty Flop,
All flew up to the cherry-tree top.
"Pooh!" said Buzzy Wuzz, "*this* is n't high!
Let us keep on till we reach the sky."

Upward they went, and they never would stop —
Fuzzy Wuzz, Buzzy Wuzz, Zipperty Flop;
"Ah, how jolly!" they started to say —
When ev'ry one of them fainted away!

The next they knew they were down on the ground,
Three dizzy bumblebees, frightened but sound;
Never a mortal had heard them drop —
Fuzzy Wuzz, Buzzy Wuzz, Zipperty Flop.

Humbled and tumbled, and dusty and lamed,
Would n't you think they 'd have been quite ashamed?
But "No, sir," they buzzed, "it was n't a fall;
We only came down from the sky, that 's all."

And now, whenever you see three bees
Buzzing and pitching about by your knees,
You 'll know, by their never once venturing high,
They 're the very same bees that flew up to the sky!

LITTLE CHARLEY

WHAT is coming? Something bright.
It fills the doorway with its light;
It thrills the room with music sweet
Of laugh and prattle and little feet;
It makes it bloom like a garden bed
With white and blue and yellow and red;
It covers the wall with pictures made
Of every moment's light and shade,
And heightens all the sunlit air
With dancing eyes and flowing hair,
Bidding our hearts sing out with joy —
And yet it 's only a little boy,
      Only our little Charley.

THE WINDMILL

SAID a hazy little, mazy little, lazy little boy:
"To see the windmill working so must every one annoy;
It can be stopped, I 'm sure it can, and I should like
  to know
What in the world can ever make a windmill want to
  go?"

Said a quizzy little, frizzy little, busy little girl:
"What can be more delightful than to see a windmill
    whirl?
It loves to go, I 'm sure it does, and hates to hang
    kerflop;
Now what on earth can ever make a windmill want
    to stop?"

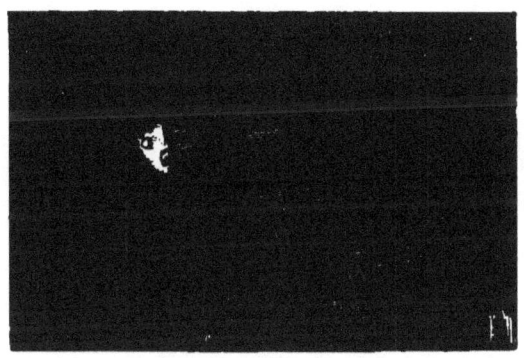

HAPPY JOHNNY; OR, TAKING LIFE
CHEERFULLY

I 'M an excellent lad, so the family say,
Because I find cheer in the gloomiest day;
For deep in my heart is this mirthful refrain,
To drive away trouble, and cure every pain:
       Tra-la-la, tra-la-la,
       Tra-la-la-la-la.

I 've a damp little room where I slumber aloof,
Where the thunder comes down, and kicks on the roof,
And the spooks slip in with a merry glide,
And coyly startle me where I hide.
       Tra-la-la, tra-la-la,
       Tra-la-la-la-la.

The bats fly in, and the light goes out,
And the social burglar prowls about—
Or I think he does—till I jump up quick,
And find he does n't, which makes me sick!
       Tra-la-la, tra-la-la,
       Tra-la-la-la-la.

The winter is full of the sport I love best,
If it were n't for the fact of a delicate chest.
And in summer, beside every daisy and tree
Malaria always is waiting for me.
       Tra-la-la, tra-la-la,
       Tra-la-la-la-la.

Now, fellows, if all of you happy would be,
Just prize your good luck, and be guided by me.
Instead of " boo-hoo "-ing, just try a " ha-ha! "
And go through the world singing tra-la-la-la,
       Tra-la-la, tra-la-la,
       Tra-la-la-la-la.

A SANTA CLAUS MESSENGER-BOY

Good morrow, my lads and lasses;
Good morrow, kind people all!
I 'm bidden by dear old Santa Claus
To make you a little call.

And, knowing your gracious courtesy,
I leave you a card to say:
" Remember the little ones of the poor
On the bountiful Christmas Day ! "

SNOWFLAKES

WHENEVER a snowflake leaves the sky,
It turns and turns to say "Good-by!
Good-by, dear clouds, so cool and gray!"
Then lightly travels on its way.

And when a snowflake finds a tree,
" Good day!" it says — "Good day to thee!
Thou art so bare and lonely, dear,
I 'll rest and call my comrades here."

But when a snowflake, brave and meek,
Lights on a rosy maiden's cheek,
It starts — "How warm and soft the day!
'T is summer!"— and it melts away.

CALLING THE FLOWERS

THE wind is shaking the old dried leaves
That will not quit their hold,
The sun slips under the stiffened grass
And drives away the cold.

Child Franca carries the dinner-horn
To summon home the men;
She raises it high for a ringing blast,
But silent it falls again.

" The men on the hill are hungry, I know,
They 've been working for hours and hours;
But first I will blow a soft note, if I can,
To call out the sweet little flowers.

" For the flowers and buds are dear little things,
And must not be frightened at all,
So pray you be gentle, you noisy old horn!—
Perhaps they will come if I call.

"Blow high for the blossoms that live in the trees,
  And low for the daisies and clover;
But as soft as I can for the violets shy,
  Yes, softly — and over and over."

PHILOPENA

ALL day the Princess ran away,
    All day the Prince ran after;
The palace grand and courtyard gray
    Rang out with silvery laughter.
"What, ho!" the King in wonder cried,
    "What ails our Princess Lena?"
"Your Majesty," the Queen replied,
    "It is the Philopena.
Our royal daughter fears to stand
Lest she take something from his hand;
The German Prince doth still pursue,
And this doth cause the sweet ado."

Then, in a lowered voice, the King:
" I 'll wage he bears a jewelled ring.
Our guest, the Prince, is brave and fair;
They 'd make, methinks, a seemly pair!"

But still the Princess ran away,
And still the Prince ran after,
While palace grand and courtyard gray
Rang out with silvery laughter.

THE MAN WHO DID N'T KNOW WHEN TO STOP

A VERY fair singer was Mynheer Schwop,
Except that he never knew when to stop;
He would sing, and sing, and sing away,
And sing half the night and all of the day—
This "pretty bit" and that "sweet air,"
This "little thing from Tootovère."
Ah! it is fearful the number he knew,
And fearful his way of singing them through.
At first, the people would kindly say:
"Ah, sing it again, Mynheer, we pray"—
(This "pretty bit," or that "sweet air,"
This "little thing from Tootovère").
They listened a while, but wearied soon,
And, like the professor, they changed their tune.
Vainly they coughed and a-hemmed and stirred;
Only the harder he trilled and slurred.
At last, in despair, and rather than grieve
The willing professor, they took their leave,
And left him singing this "sweet air,"
And that "pretty bit from Tootovère";

Until the host turned down the light,
With "Thanks, Mynheer! Good night! good night!"

My moral, dear singers, lies plainly a-top:
Be always obliging, and willing — to stop.
The same will apply, my dear children, to you;
Whenever you 've any performing to do,
Your friends to divert (which is quite proper, too),
Do the best that you can — *and stop when you 're
through.*

THE OREGON EXPRESS

ALL aboard for Oregon!
Fayelle, Gertrude, Charley, John,
Kern, and Emily—Dolly too;
Frank, the dog, has joined the crew.
Don't you hear the whistle blow?
That 's to start the train, you know.
Kern, the daring engineer,
Brave and quick, scorns every fear.
Ding, dong! clear the track!
There 's a cow! They 'll have to back!
Soon they 're at the signal-bar,
And a wicker parlor-car—
Baby Karl's — is coupled on.
Now they 're off for Oregon.
" Tick—*ets!*" shouts Conductor John.

Home again, by light of day;
All to sup with Kern and Fay.

HOW WILLY'S SHIP CAME BACK

Willy, our bonny sailor,
 With a " Hi-ho!" and a " Heave away!"
Willy, our would-be whaler,
" Oho, lads, ho!"

Ruddy of cheek and eager-eyed,
 Willy, our sailor boy:
Ship-builder he of a tiny craft,
Hear him, our whaler boy:

"My, but the boat was a beauty!
 A staver! A stunning toy!
And all by myself I built her."
(Willy, our sailor boy.)

" She was n't more than a handful,
 That, sir, I don't deny;
But she went on a voyage of wonder
 And came back high and dry.

" She sailed from the pool like a good one,
 And then she slipped from sight,

Dipped, in a flash, and was gone, sir!"
(Willy, our midshipmite!)

"Then up she rose on a billow,
And sailed till I lost her track;
I waited, and waited, and waited,—
And how do you think she came back?"

Willy, our bonny sailor,
  With a "Hi-ho!" and a "Heave away!"
Willy, our would-be whaler,
  "Oho, lads, ho!"

"I heard a frisking and dashing,
Soft as the lightest spray,
A tittering crowd came splashing
To the cool rock where I lay.

"Up I sprang in a hurry.
Oh, but I saw a sight!
Six queer, bright little faces,
Dripping and merry with light.

"They were mermaids, sure as I 'm living,
Bringing my boat to me,
That mite of a boat;—now I 'm giving
The story as straight as can be!

"They clung, their bright hair streaming,
Close to my rock, and laughed;

Now why do you think I was dreaming?
And why do you say I was daft?

" The boat,— where is it? you wonder?
Well, somehow, before I knew,
The mermaids and boat slipped under,
And hid in the waters blue."

Willy, our bonny sailor,
With a " Hi-ho!" and a " Heave away!"
Willy, our bold young whaler,
" Oho, lads, ho!"

A STIR AMONG THE DAISIES

PRETTY Lill of Littleton sauntered through the grass;
The very birds and butterflies stopped to see her pass;
  All the daisies nodded to the maiden coming by,
    And leaned across the pathway left behind her.
  "Art hurt?" they asked each other. Each gaily
    laughed, "Not I!
  We bowed too low; but really we don't mind her.
To see so fair a maiden pass has really quite unstrung us;
But we 'll straighten up, and ready be when next she
    comes among us."

THE LITTLE KINDERGARTEN GIRL

IF we sew, sew, sew, and pull, pull, pull,
The pattern will come and the card be full;
So it 's criss, criss, criss, and it 's cross, cross, cross;
If we have some pleasant work to do we 're never
　at a loss.

Oh, dear!   I pulled too roughly — I 've broken
   through my card.
I feel like throwing all away, and crying pretty hard.
But no, no, no, — for we never should despair,
So I 'll rip, rip, rip, and I 'll tear, tear, tear.

There! you pretty purple worsted, I 've saved you
   every stitch
(Because if we are wasteful we never can get rich).
Now I 'll start another tablet, and I 'll make it perfect
   yet,
And Mother 'll say, " Oh, thank you, my precious
   little pet!"

HOW SHOCKING!

My grandma met a fair gallant one day,
And, blushing, gave the gentleman a daisy.
Now, if *your* grandma acted in that way,
Would you not think the dear old soul was crazy?
O — h, *Grandmama!*

And then the gentleman bent smiling down,
And told my grandma that he loved her dearly;
And Grandma, smiling back, forgot to frown,
— Ah, Grandpa nods! So he recalls it clearly?
O — h, *Grandpapa!*

"LITTLE POT SOON HOT"

Fume and fury! I have cause
To tear about and break the laws.

But, on the whole, I 'd better not;
"Little pots are soon hot."

Little souls slights discover;
Big souls pass 'em over.

Big souls bear their trouble;
Little souls sizz and bubble.

Little souls oft ferment;
Big souls are content.

Big souls tumble slowly;
Little souls — roly poly!

Big souls, like as not,
When it 's fitting, *do* get hot.

But "little pots" all grandeur spoil.
I 'll think a bit before I boil!

THE BICYCLE BOYS

I

Oh, the bicycle boys,
The bicycle boys!
They care not for tops
Or babyish toys;
They 're done with their hobbies
And that sort of play,
As mounted on nothing
They 're off, and away!

II

Oh, the bicycle boys,
The bicycle boys!
They travel along
Without any noise.
They travel so softly,
They travel so fast,
They always get somewhere,
I 'm told, at the last.

III

They race with each other,
They race with a horse,
All sure they will beat
As a matter of course;
And often they win,
And often they fall; —
Then "down comes bicycle,
Boy, and all!"

LITTLE ROSY RED-CHEEK

Little Rosy Red-cheek said unto a clover:
" Flower, why were you made?
I was made for mother,
She has n't any other;
But you were made for no one, I 'm afraid."

Then the clover softly unto Red-cheek whispered:
" Pluck me, ere you go."
Red-cheek, little dreaming,
Pulled, and ran off screaming,
" Oh, naughty, naughty flower, to sting me so!"

" Foolish child!" the startled bee buzzed crossly,
" Foolish not to see
That I make my honey
While the day is sunny;
That the pretty little clover lives for me!"

NOW THE NOISY WINDS ARE STILL

Now the noisy winds are still
April's coming up the hill!
All the spring is in her train,
Led by shining ranks of rain:
  Pit, pat, patter, patter,
  Sudden sun, and clatter, clatter!—
First the blue, and then the shower,
Bursting bud, and smiling flower,

Brooks set free with tinkling ring;
Birds too full of song to sing;
Dry old leaves astir with pride,
Where the timid violets hide,—
All things ready with a will,—
April's coming up the hill!

NOT ONLY IN THE CHRISTMAS-TIDE

Not only in the Christmas-tide
   The holy baby lay;
But month by month his home he blessed,
   And brightened every day.

Each season held its light divine,
   Its glow of love and cheer;
For Christ, who lived for all the world,
   Was part of all the year.

IN TRUST

It 's coming, boys,
  It 's almost here;
It 's coming, girls,
  The grand New Year!
A year to be glad in,
Not to be bad in,
A year to live in,
To gain and give in;
A year for trying
And not for sighing;
A year for striving,
And hearty thriving;
A bright New Year,
Oh! hold it dear;
For God, who sendeth,
He only lendeth.

www.ingramcontent.com/pod-product-compliance
Lightning Source LLC
Chambersburg PA
CBHW020050030726

47498CB00006B/1717